SUGAR SENTRY

SUGAR DADDIES #13

CHARITY PARKERSON

--Warning: This book is intended for readers over the age of 18.

Copyright © 2019 Charity Parkerson
Editor: Hercules Editing & Consultants
ISBN: 978-1-946099-50-1

INTRODUCTION

EASTON'S BEEN LIVING ONE DAY AT A TIME SINCE
HIS ATTACK. LIFE HAS OTHER PLANS FOR HIM.

Exactly one year ago, Easton's life came crashing down. A vicious attack left him deeply scarred inside and out. From the ashes of his life, he's rebuilt himself into someone new. His life is different in many ways, but—mostly—he's found a better version of happiness in a new business. Opening his own bakery has been a lifesaver for him. He's thrown himself into becoming a massive success. For the most part, he's content. Until Nico walks in and shakes the foundation of Easton's newfound peace.

After a year of watching over Easton from a distance, Nico has decided to take on a more hands-on approach. Easton is getting better, but he's not really living, and Nico can't put up with that anymore.

He's decided to take his self-imposed guardianship role to the next level and lure Easton out of his fear-encased shell. There are just a few problems with his plan. He loves Easton, Easton doesn't think he deserves love, and Nico is carrying around one hell of a secret that could ruin everything.

Author Note

I'm hoping you've read every book in the series leading up to Easton's. If so, you can pretty much guess that Easton's story will have triggers.

ONE

AT TEN TILL NINE, on the one-year anniversary of the night he'd almost died, Easton questioned why he'd decided to stay open so late. Maybe it had been some type of silent punishment. When he'd opened Easton's Bakery, he'd never intended to stay open past six. He'd just wanted a tiny bakery with a small area where people could choose to stay, eat some pie or whatever, and enjoy a bit of quiet time. Unfortunately, he'd seriously misjudged how many people would place huge orders they couldn't pick up until after work. Easton couldn't complain about the success. He'd never dreamed he'd make it this far. In fact, for many years, he never had much of a dream for himself at all. He'd spent his entire life looking for validation from men. Now he owned his own business. Mostly thanks to his brother, Jake, and Jake's husband, Flynn, building on to their bookstore for him, but he'd done a lot to make the place a success. It was doing amazingly well. He should be thrilled. Most days, he was. Except when it came to this. This day on the calendar had changed Easton—inside and out. Now, it was dark outside; he was alone and scared to death of walking to his car alone. Just as he'd been that night a year ago.

Easton pressed his hand to his stomach, trying to stop the shaking. His gaze moved to the clock on the register. Five more minutes. The door opened and a warm breeze blew in, stirring the air and pulling Easton from his rising panic. He should be irritated over someone coming in right at closing time. All Easton felt was relief for the reprieve.

He pasted on a fake smile. "Welcome to Easton's." His bright tone faltered as he caught his first glimpse of the man. Fear choked him. His gaze hit the counter. Easton had a hard time lifting his eyes. The guy was massive. His muscles were thick and hard. Tattoos ran down the length of one arm, covered his neck, and even showed beneath his close-shaven hair. He looked like he'd stumbled into the wrong side of town. Easton had never felt smaller.

He couldn't claim he'd never been more vulnerable, but he definitely didn't feel safe. He kept his hands curled into fists so the man wouldn't see how they shook. Easton had told Jake he would be fine on his own while Jake and his husband were out of town. Now, as he ground his back teeth to a fine dust, he wished he hadn't lied.

"How can I help you?" His voice came out sounding small. Easton forced himself to lift his chin and meet the man's stare. His eyes automatically skirted away. The guy's eyes were like blue ice. They were so light, they were almost unnatural.

"Are you Easton?"

Easton gave a jerky nod as his gaze collided with the blue ice and jumped away again.

"Everyone tells me you are the best. What do you suggest? What are you most proud of?"

He tried following. The man's thick Russian accent made it hard for Easton to understand him. Easton turned the words over in his head. A hint of pride sneaked in. Someone had recommended him. This guy wanted whatever Easton thought was his best creation. He straightened his spine.

"My five-layer chocolate cake is really popular, but it's extremely rich. If you're not a fan of super sweet cakes, I'd go with a lemon cupcake with strawberry icing. It's that one," he said, pointing at a pink creation he thought had turned out really pretty.

"Do you have coffee?"

Usually, he did, but it was late. "Not made, but if you wanted to wait, I could start a pot."

He dipped his chin. "I wait. Coffee, chocolate cake, and I take the pink thing to go."

The guy was gruff and scary-looking, but he was spending money. Easton told himself he would be okay. "Can I get a name for your order?" Easton kind of wanted to slap himself. It was closing time. No one else was there. The question had become pure habit.

The guy didn't question him. "Nico."

Easton nodded. He moved to the register and rang up his purchases. "Fourteen thirty-seven."

Nico pulled a wad of cash out of his pocket so thick, it had to look like a second dick filling his pants. Easton hoped it wasn't drug money. He would still take it, but he hoped. Nico peeled a fifty from the stack. "The change is yours."

Easton's eyebrows snapped together. "Are you sure? That's too much."

Nico stared him down in stony silence.

His bravery fled again. Easton dropped his chin

and counted out the change. He slipped the extra bills in his pocket before turning away to make the coffee.

"Good boy." Nico's softly spoken praise almost made Easton miss a step. No one praised him and meant it. To hear those words from someone so intimidating was odd and messed with him a little.

Easton went through the motions, cutting Nico a slice of cake before moving to start the coffee. Nico never budged. He was so still, it was almost as if he wasn't real. Easton felt like a fumbling mess. Nico was just big. That was the heart of things. He was a stranger and in Easton's space. Easton didn't want to be this person who was scared of every new encounter, but he didn't know how to make it stop. The nightmares that came without warning. The night sweats when the panic attacks hit. Those were his new reality. Jake and Flynn had paid for counseling for Easton after the attack. It helped, but he was different now. All Easton could do was try to brazen this out.

He set the plate in front of Nico and moved to box up his cupcake. Easton spoke over his shoulder as he worked. "Your coffee should be ready soon. Do you need sugar and cream?"

"Black is good."

Easton curled his nose. He'd never understood how anyone drank black coffee. This guy planned to drink it black at almost nine at night. Insane. He glanced up. A small smile hovered on Nico's lips. It disappeared when he noticed Easton looking. With a shake of his head, Easton carried the cake box over and set it next to Nico's plate. A whiff of expensive cologne overcame him, making Easton miss a step. There was something familiar about the scent. He probed at his memories, trying to shake something loose without luck as he poured a cup of coffee. When he turned to hand the cup to Nico, his plate was empty, even though he hadn't sat or even moved as far as Easton could tell.

"*Danke.*"

Oh. The accent wasn't Russian. It was German. His voice was deep, and Easton had never been good at telling accents apart. For all his expensive tastes, Easton had never cared for world travel. Not every country appreciated beautiful and sassy men like him. Easton's thoughts skipped a beat and reversed. Sometimes, when his mind wandered, he forgot he wasn't beautiful any longer. Easton dropped his gaze and avoided turning his scars in Nico's direction.

"Can I do anything else for you?"

"No."

With a nod, Easton moved away. He wiped down the counters and boxed up the day's leftovers. In his head, he ran down the list of everything he needed to do before he could go home. In truth, he was stalling. His car wasn't parked that far away. It didn't matter. Easton always had a panic attack the second he stepped outside alone. Sometimes he thought he'd never get better. The flashbacks would never stop.

He stacked the cake boxes filled with leftovers to give his hands something to do. Easton pulled the knot loose on his apron. He tugged the pink cloth over his head and draped it over a hook by the kitchen door. With nothing else to keep him from facing the inevitable, he took a deep breath and turned. Nico still hadn't moved. It was funny. He'd forgotten the man was there. Nico was so still and quiet. Nonetheless, Easton couldn't believe he'd forgotten. Being around men made him uncomfortable. Normally, he always knew exactly how far he stood from every stranger. As terrifying as Nico was, he should've been twice as hard to forget.

Nico's cup was empty. Easton carried the dishes to the sink, hoping Nico would take the hint. It was well past closing time. Easton turned back toward the counter. Nico held the cake boxes filled with leftovers. Easton blinked in surprise.

"It is dark. I walk you out."

"Oh." Easton barely stopped himself from snatching the boxes away and screeching like a wildcat. His heart raced. "You don't have to do that."

Nico didn't budge. His face was set. Easton eyed the man's cold eyes and the thick brown hair covering his jaw. He looked unmoving. Fuck it. The guy couldn't carry boxes and kill him. Yeah, it was a thin theory, but Easton wouldn't make it if he thought too hard to the contrary.

Easton grabbed his keys and nodded toward the door. "After you, I guess."

Nico headed for the door. Easton eyed his massive frame as they headed out. He swallowed. Nico probably wouldn't need both hands to kill him. He looked like he could hold cake boxes in one hand and snap Easton's neck with the other. With each step, Easton's panic rose. His hands shook. He pulled the door closed behind them and tried locking the door. The keys rattled in his hand. Easton bit his lip, trying to force his hands to steady. Nico shifted the boxes to one arm, plucked the keys from Easton's fingers, and locked the door. Easton stared hard in the opposite direction. He felt like an idiot. No doubt he looked like a goddamn scared mouse. He hated being like this.

"Is this your car?" Nico asked, pulling Easton from his deepening depression.

Easton glanced toward his Audi. It was a few years old. A gift from a former lover. No one would date him now much less shower him with expensive gifts. An unexpected wave of unhappiness washed over Easton. His bakery had been a dream come true, but everything else had fallen apart in a single night a year ago. He was very tired.

"Yeah. That's me." There was a Harley parked next to his car. Easton motioned toward the bike. "Is that you?" He didn't know why he asked. Silence wasn't comfortable for him.

Nico nodded. He didn't waste words, apparently.

Easton swiped his sweating palms on his thighs. "Well, you've walked me out," Easton said, hoping Nico took the hint and gave back his keys.

Nico dipped his chin again and headed for Easton's car. He unlocked it and opened the door for Easton. "You will be fine." It was such an odd thing to say. Easton automatically moved to Nico's side and slipped behind the wheel. Nico leaned down and passed the boxes to Easton. While Easton set them in the passenger side seat, Nico started the car for Easton. He hit the button, locking Easton's door. Without a word, he closed the door and walked away. Easton sat there blinking. He had no clue what the fuck just happened to his life.

TWO

NICO DELIBERATELY WAITED until five minutes until closing to show up at Easton's again. As he came through the door, the smell of cake and books combined to smack him in the face. Easton looked his way. Unlike the night before, Easton didn't immediately drop his gaze. His eyes were fucking amazing up close. The bravery he showed, defiantly holding Nico's stare a few seconds at a time, proved Easton was a warrior. Whether he realized it or not.

"You're back. Does that mean you liked my cake?"

Honestly, Nico didn't particularly like sweets. He preferred things salty. "What are you proud of today?"

Easton smiled. Nico sucked in a breath. This wasn't the fake smile Easton gave while greeting customers. His smile was genuine, filled with happiness, pride, and teasing. Nico was famished. "I tried my hand at something new today. Would you like to try it?"

"If it pleases you, ja."

Easton's smile turned shy. "It's salted caramel cinnamon rolls. Would you like some coffee too?"

Nico nodded as he pulled out some money and handed Easton a fifty as he'd done last night. "The change is for you."

For a moment, Easton hesitated. Nico worried he was getting ready to argue again. Instead, Easton kept his head down and counted out the change. He slipped the money in his pocket. "Thanks." He still didn't look Nico's way as he scooped a roll onto a plate and poured a cup of coffee. He set them in front of Nico. "So... coffee at night. You must stay up late. I don't have a very high tolerance for caffeine. One cup after lunch and I'm up all night, bouncing from the walls."

"This is a small cup and I'm a big guy. This is nothing. Let me guess, you are a wine drinker."

Easton shoved his hands in his back pockets and rocked from foot to foot. He still didn't look directly at Nico for more than a few seconds at a time, but a smile hovered on his lips. His nose curled in an adorable way at Nico's stab in the dark. "No. My family belongs to this country club and everyone there claims to be an expert on all the best wines. I'd never have to work again if I had a dollar for every time I've said I don't like the taste of alcohol and someone there said, 'that's because you haven't tried so and so yet.' Elitists are exhausting."

He did such a good job of impersonating a snooty rich voice that Nico couldn't help but laugh. "No coffee before noon and no wine ever. What do you drink?"

A blush touched Easton's cheeks. His gaze skirted away again. "I guess I'm somewhat boring. Usually, I just drink water."

"You don't look boring." Nico shoved a bite of cinnamon roll in his mouth before he looked like he was flirting. He'd kept his tone steady, but he worried about scaring Easton. The man was already one wrong word from bolting.

Easton flashed him a crooked smile. "How do I look?" He swiped his hand through the air and blushed again. "Don't answer that. I know how I look." He covered the scarred side of his face and laughed. There was no humor in the sound, even though Nico got the feeling Easton still intended the words as a joke. It was obvious Easton wanted to laugh about his injuries, but it would never be funny.

"You look feisty." Nico infused a good dose of humor in his voice, hoping to keep Easton's spirits up. He couldn't say what he really thought. Easton looked like a beautiful warrior. A conqueror angel. A fighter.

Easton released a loud bark of laughter. He slapped his hand over his mouth. His blush deepened. Nico's smile grew until his cheeks ached.

With a final shake of his head, as if he thought Nico's claim was ridiculous, Easton turned away and started his normal end-of-the-day routine. Wiping down the counters one final time, taking off his apron, and boxing up the day's leftovers. Nico polished off his cinnamon roll and blatantly watched. Easton moved as if he'd forgotten anyone else was there—like music played inside his head. Nico marveled over Easton's spark. He had something others didn't. It fascinated Nico how Easton could be so full of light and energy, yet he didn't live. Not really.

Just as he'd done last night, Easton turned and startled slightly, as if he'd truly forgotten Nico's presence. "You're so still and quiet. I get lost in thought and forget you're here." He winced. "Sorry."

Nico didn't want Easton's apologies. He liked knowing he could stare at Easton without the guilt of making him uncomfortable. "It's raining tonight."

Easton snagged his dishes. He pulled a face. "Is it? It's so dark, I hadn't noticed."

"You will be safe." Nico lifted his umbrella just enough for Easton to see.

Another shy smile passed over Easton's lips. "Thanks. I didn't bring one today. I'm terrible at remembering to check the weather." He was getting more comfortable with Nico by the moment. Nico swore he could feel the tension leaking from Easton a tiny bit at a time. "Would you like anything else before we go?"

Nico slid from the barstool. "I'm ready." He waited on Easton to gather his things. When Easton picked up the stack of cupcake boxes, Nico nodded toward him. "What do you do with all those? You're so tiny." Like a delicious little snack, Nico added silently. "I can't image you sitting home, polishing off all the cakes."

Easton laughed. It was such a sweet sound. Nico couldn't look away. "Definitely not. I could, but I'd end up with diabetes. If I thought I'd gain some weight or it would make me taller, I might try it. I've been the same size since I was fourteen."

He did look very young and tiny for his age. Easton was like a pixie. Tiny and sparkly. "Your small size is good."

Easton shot him a questioning glance.

Nico smiled. "You won't take up much space beneath the umbrella."

With a chuckle, Easton headed for the door. Nico measured his steps, ensuring he didn't hover too close and make Easton nervous. He opened the umbrella as Easton opened the door. Nico didn't want to risk Easton getting wet before he could get him covered.

"That's bad luck, you know? Opening an umbrella inside."

"Why?"

For a moment, Easton stared at him and blinked. A luminous smile exploded across his face, taking Nico's breath away. "I have no idea. Someone probably came up with that to stop kids from playing inside with them and putting someone's eye out. That's definitely something my mother would've done. God forbid my brother or I ever have any fun."

Nico's chest still felt tight from Easton's smile. It took him a second to realize the man had actually told him something about himself without prodding. It was progress.

With a shake of his head, as if still puzzling Nico's question, Easton stepped outside. Nico crowded his space and kept him safe from the pouring rain. With the door locked, Easton faced him once again. They were inches apart while trying to stay dry. Easton smelled amazing. Nico took measured breaths, fighting the urge to show his hand. Water poured down his back as he kept most of the umbrella over Easton. Nico didn't care. Clothes would dry. He'd never have this moment again.

"I take them to the hospital staff each morning."

Nico blinked. He had no idea what Easton meant.

Thankfully, Easton didn't force him to ask. He nodded at the boxes he held, reminding Nico of his earlier question. "The nurses and staff at Coastline Medical work crazy hours. It brightens their day to get free snacks. They took amazing care of me last year." He motioned absently to his face. "When this happened. This is the least I can do." *When this happened*—like it had been an accident and not intentional. Nico wished he didn't know the truth. Before Nico could form a response, Easton turned, took one step, and froze. "Holy shit. Is that your car?"

Nico set his hand on the small of Easton's back without thought, keeping him moving. "Ja."

Easton glanced over, smiling. He didn't jump away from Nico's touch, so Nico didn't stop. "I had this exact car when I was eighteen. It was a graduation gift. I had to sell it a couple of years ago for… reasons, but I loved it. It was my baby."

Nico smirked, fighting back a wave of pride. "Sixty-seven was a good year for Mustang. Would you like to go for a ride?"

Easton's smile faltered. His gaze slid away. "Maybe some other time."

He could feel Easton rebuilding his walls. Nico couldn't lose the footing he'd gained. "What if I let you drive? You'll be the one in control." The way Easton's gaze shyly slid back his way had hope rising in Nico's chest. He kept pushing. "Just two blocks. You can see my shop as we drive past."

"You own a shop?"

Nico nodded.

Easton's smile reappeared. "Okay." He immediately bit his lip as if he couldn't decide if he should take it back.

Nico didn't give him time. He maneuvered Easton to the driver's side, unlocked the door, and handed him the keys. Once he had Easton settled behind the wheel, he circled the car and waited until Easton leaned over and tugged up the lock.

Laughter filled the car as Nico slid inside. "I forgot what it was like for nothing to be electric. I almost left you standing out in the rain." Easton waited until Nico dropped the umbrella in the floor before passing his cake boxes over. Nico reached over the seat and set them in the back. His gaze refused to budge from Easton as he adjusted the seat.

Easton eyed the mirrors. "Is it okay if I move these? It'll take you forever to get everything back the way you like it."

"It's good. Do what you need. I only drive this car on occasion."

The way Easton never stopped smiling as he fixed the mirrors and started the car had hunger rising in Nico. Easton put the car in reverse. His mischievous green gaze slid Nico's way. "Are you ready?"

Nico gave him a short nod.

Easton's smile grew as he backed from the lot. "You've done some work to this car. I'm pretty sure this one is way more powerful than the one I had."

"It's my job. You look happy."

A soft chuckle filled the air. "I feel like I'm eighteen again. What do you mean it's your job?"

"My business is a car shop. I fix up old cars, making them faster, louder, and gorgeous." While Easton kept his gaze locked on the road, Nico stayed locked on him, watching. Waiting.

Easton cocked his head to one side. "Wait. You said two blocks. You don't own Stylin' Rides on Oak Way, do you?"

Nico smiled. "That's me."

"That place is behind the club I..." He visibly took a breath. "I thought that place was owned by some famous boxer. It was on the news."

"Retired boxer."

Easton glanced over. "Seriously?" He looked away. "I can see it."

Nico bit the inside of cheek to keep from laughing. "Now you know where I work. In case you wish to come in right at closing time and stop me from leaving on time someday."

A bark of loud laughter escaped Easton. He covered his mouth. The move bothered Nico.

"Why do you do this?"

"Do what?" Easton asked, casting him another quick glance.

"Smother your laughs."

The way Easton kept his gaze locked on the road was telling. He didn't want to answer. "Habit, I guess. Over the years, almost everyone I've spent time with didn't like for me to be too loud. I was for show. Not anymore," he said, tossing a self-deprecating smile as he motioned toward his scars.

That was bullshit. Nico didn't say it. "You said almost everyone."

Easton nodded. He made a U-turn before responding. When he did, he sounded reluctant. "I dated someone nice once, but I was super young. Eighteen. Just out of high school. We were together seven years. He started dropping hints about getting married and I panicked. I realized I hadn't done anything. I had no dreams that were mine. As soon as I graduated, I moved from my parents' house to his. I felt cornered, so I completely destroyed everything. You'd be surprised how very good I am at taking a sledgehammer to my life."

"And now?"

"Now what?"

Nico could hear the smile in Easton's voice. "You've found your dream now, right? No one can tell you to be silent. You should laugh as loud as you want. I like your laugh."

"That's a nice thing to say." Easton pulled into the parking spot next to his car again. They both went for the cake boxes at the same time. Their faces were inches apart. Up close, Easton was even more beautiful than Nico had ever imagined. He looked young and fragile. Nico wished for one kiss. A blush touched Easton's cheeks. He moved away, freeing Nico from his spell. "Sorry. It's probably easier for you to reach." He ran his hand around the steering wheel in a show of nerves. "Thank you for letting me feel young again for a few minutes. She drives like a dream."

"Easton." Even Nico heard the longing in the sound of Easton's name.

Easton glanced over, looking ready to bolt.

Nico took a breath, trying to stop himself from scaring Easton. He wasn't unaware of his intensity. "Tomorrow night, you will ride my Harley."

"Okay." Easton's immediate acceptance had Nico fighting back a triumphant crow. Baby steps. He was inching toward breaking down Easton's walls. Tomorrow couldn't get here fast enough. He already couldn't wait to see Easton again.

THREE

FOR THE TENTH time in the last half an hour, Easton forced himself to stop chewing his nails. Nico was coming back tonight. He didn't know why he was damn nervous about it. It wasn't like it was a date. Nico was just a customer. Maybe he was becoming a regular, but that was where things ended. He didn't know why Nico stayed to walk him out or let Easton drive his car. Easton definitely didn't understand why Nico demanded Easton go for a ride with him tonight. He didn't think it was a romantic interest or anything like that. Easton didn't get that vibe. Maybe the guy was just lonely. It was hard to make friends as an adult. They were both business owners and had the same taste in cars. Shit. He shouldn't be so nervous.

Easton caught a glimpse of himself in the printed mirror above the bar. As always, his gaze went straight to the scars marring his face. Easton never looked in the mirror and just saw himself any longer. He was nothing more than the nightmare he'd endured. There were dark smudges beneath his eyes from where he no longer slept. Most nights, he paced the floor of the bedroom he'd been assigned inside his brother's home. Everything had been stolen from him in a single night. He could afford to live on his own, but he probably never would again. Unless Jake or Flynn put him out, that is. Easton lived with that constant fear. Without thought, Easton's gaze dropped to his hands. Fine white scars covered his knuckles from where he'd fought for his life. He lifted his shirt and eyed the marks on his stomach before he lost his nerve and dropped the material. Easton couldn't let his mind form the memory of the knife carving at his skin. He could barely stand to see himself nude. His body was now a prison no one would ever want. Not that it mattered. Inside, he was an even bigger mess. He'd probably come completely unglued if anyone tried touching him. The most traitorous thought of all sneaked in, the way it always did at his lowest. Maybe he'd gotten exactly what he deserved that night. Maybe Karma had finally come calling.

"What are you most proud of tonight?"

Easton's gaze snapped up, colliding with ice-blue eyes. For a moment, his mind stayed trapped in that ugly place where life had finally served him the only dish he'd earned. He blinked. The fear gripping his throat eased. There was something about Nico's eyes. Something that washed away the panic. He was safe.

"I'm afraid there's not much left over today. Business was pretty steady all day long. I have a blueberry muffin, one slice of carrot cake, and two red velvet cupcakes."

"Coffee?"

Easton's mouth lifted one corner. "Just for you." He poured Nico a cup while chewing his bottom lip and trying not to smile. Easton was ridiculously happy to see Nico for no reason at all. He set the cup in front of him. "How was your day?"

"Long."

"Mine too. I had a doctor's appointment before I opened. That made it feel even longer. What made your day so lengthy?"

Nico stared at him in silence for so long, Easton

almost asked if he wanted to be left alone with his coffee. "Impatience," he said finally.

Easton wanted to ask more, but he was scared. Easton decided not to push Nico to talk. He knew most men liked it better when he was quiet. The problem was, he didn't really have anything to do. He'd been so excited and nervous, he'd already cleaned everything there was to clean, and ditched his apron. His gaze wandered while he waited for Nico to finish his drink.

"How much do I owe?"

Easton's gaze jumped back to Nico. The cup was still full. "It's on me tonight."

Nico stood. "Are you ready to go?"

Confusion had Easton furrowing his brow. "You didn't finish your drink."

"I didn't pay for it."

Easton took a breath, trying not to sigh. Nico was so stubborn. Easton counted to five in his head. "Did you want the coffee?"

"No."

For some reason, a smile exploded across Easton's face. Nico was strange and slightly maddening. It was like breathing fresh air. "Then I'm ready."

Nico fell into step beside him as he headed for

the door. His palm collided with the small of Easton's back. Easton didn't move away. Nico's touch didn't feel threatening. In fact, as large and scary as Nico looked, he made Easton feel safe and protected. It was comforting. He hadn't felt that way in a long time.

After locking up, Easton headed for the motorcycle—determined. "Okay. What do I need to do?"

An odd expression crossed Nico's face. "Have you never been on a bike?"

Easton shrugged. "What can I say? I told you I'm boring."

"No. You're not." Nico's denial was calm and sure—like he knew something Easton didn't. He unstrapped a helmet from the bike and moved to stand over Easton. Without preamble, Nico plopped the helmet on his head and adjusted the strap. Easton wondered if he looked like a little kid standing next to Nico's huge frame. With Easton secure, Nico strapped on his own helmet and tossed one leg over the bike, straddling it. "Climb on."

Easton felt like an idiot—like he was climbing on for a piggyback ride. Somehow, he managed. He got the feeling his ascent looked every bit as ungraceful as it felt, but he was on.

"Put your arms around me and hold on."

Easton shifted closer and wrapped his arms around Nico. The moment his palms landed on rock solid abs, his brain misfired. He bit his tongue to keep from saying something stupid in his shock. He shouldn't have been surprised. Nico was a retired professional boxer. It made sense he'd be in good shape. Knowing it and feeling it were two distinctly different things.

"Don't let go."

"Okay." Fuck. He sounded way too chipper. Easton needed to reel it in. They were just friends and Easton was damaged. Even the average man wouldn't be interested in Easton now. Easton didn't stand a chance with someone like Nico. Plus, the man wasn't his type, even if nothing stood in the way. Back when Easton actually dated, he'd only dated doctors and lawyers. Stock brokers. A sick feeling ate at Easton's gut. The unhappiness he'd felt every single day back then washed over Easton at just the memory of who he'd once been. It had taken losing himself to find himself. Too bad he'd discovered his true self too late for it to matter. Easton didn't plan to ever date again. Not only did he have nothing to offer, no one had anything to offer him either. He was fine alone. Even as the thought crossed his mind,

Easton caught himself stroking Nico's hard stomach. He forced his hands still. This was just a ride. Nothing more.

Nico peeled out. A laugh tore from Easton's throat. His arms tightened around Nico, holding on for dear life. It was a bit freeing. His teeth shook from the vibration. He was terrified and one wrong move away from death, but he was having a blast. When Nico hit the interstate, he really opened her up, forcing Easton to mold against Nico's back. Fifteen minutes later, Nico hit the exit and headed toward the bluffs. Easton fought the urge to question him. He'd thought they were only going for a quick ride. Nico seemed to have other plans. He pulled over at a carnival overlooking the ocean. Easton didn't let go, even when Nico killed the bike.

Nico took off his helmet and looked over his shoulder. "You will be fine."

It was easily the third time Nico had said those words to him. Easton couldn't explain why he took it in the chest every single time. He forced his arms to move and climbed off the bike. Easton tried taking off the helmet by himself with no luck. His fight ended in an aggravated huff when the strap wouldn't budge. Nico laughed. Easton's breath caught. He couldn't look away as Nico closed the distance between them, smiling. He had laugh lines around his eyes and dimples. Easton didn't as much as blink as Nico helped him out of the helmet. He prayed he didn't look as dumbfounded as he felt. Easton did not want to see Nico in the light he was currently seeing.

"When was the last time you went to carnival?"

Easton shook his head, trying to shake off the spell. "I've never been."

Nico froze in the middle of strapping the helmets to the bike. "What? That is no good. You must act the kid and forget these rides are death's trap. You will ride with me."

"Okay." God help him. Easton worried he'd agree to any suggestion that rolled from Nico's tongue. Even he didn't know why. All Easton knew was, Nico took away the fear that choked him all hours of the day. He needed the friendship Nico offered. Maybe Nico needed him too. One could hope because—it seemed—that was one thing that hadn't died alongside Easton's old self.

Nico forced Easton onto every ride, even when he swore the last one almost killed him. With every smile and laugh, Nico tried for another.

Between showing off his manliness in the rigged games and trying several fried foods, there was laughter and talking. Just talking. Easton was a happy chatterer. He spoke with his hands. In fact, he was the most animated person Nico ever met. The night wasn't without its rough patches. There were times when people stood too close and a wild look entered Easton's eyes. In those moments, Nico would silently crowd Easton's space, using his size to block Easton from sight. He wanted to tell Easton he'd keep him safe. No one would harm him again. It was harder than he expected, pretending he didn't notice or know.

"Are you tired?"

Easton looked over at Nico's question. His eyes shone bright with happiness. "No. I should be. I've been going since eight this morning." He shrugged. "But I'm good."

"Let me have this one," Nico said, plucking the rainbow-colored bear he'd won from Easton's arms. He strapped the bear to the back of the bike so they wouldn't lose him. "There. He is good." With the bear secured, Nico dug through his saddlebag and found a thin blanket. "Let's go." He held his hand out to Easton without thought. To his surprise, Easton linked fingers with him and let Nico pull him into the darkness and away from the crowd. Hand in hand, they made their way closer to the bluffs and farther away from the lights and noise. When he'd gone far enough to satisfy his need for privacy, Nico spread out the blanket and fell across it in a heap. He linked his fingers behind his head and stared up at Easton.

With a shrug, Easton joined him. Rather than settling in beside him, Easton turned sideways and used Nico's stomach as a pillow. Easton stared at the sky. Nico stared at Easton.

"I don't think I've really looked at the stars in years."

"Why did you stop?" Because Nico needed to know every thought Easton had. He'd watched too long from a distance. Cared more than he should for a stranger.

He felt Easton shrug. "When I was a kid, I honest to god believed in wishing on the brightest star. I was absolutely certain, if I wished hard enough, the stars would see my desperation and give me what I wanted. There's only so long you can hold on to things like that before disillusion sets in and you never look up again."

"What did you want so badly?"

Easton crossed his arms over his chest as if

protecting his heart. Nico swore he could feel Easton's discomfort. "It's dumb. I was just a kid."

Nico stroked Easton's hair, because he had to know how it felt. "I promise not to laugh. You were, as you said, a kid. Everyone has been there with the innocent mind and wishes."

"I wished that I would die." Easton said the words fast, like ripping off a bandage.

In his career, Nico had taken a lot of hits. He'd never been sucker punched in the chest so hard. Before he could think of a single response, Easton chuckled. There was no real humor in the sound. It was obvious he meant to laugh off his statement.

"I was a dramatic kid. Whenever life didn't go my way, I could cry at the drop of a hat. Then, my brother, Jake, would make sure I got whatever I wanted by calmly bargaining with my parents. Since they wanted nothing more than for him to be a great lawyer—like them—they gave in if he had a sound argument." Easton took a breath. When he spoke again, Nico could hear the smile in his voice. "Then I hit my teenage years and grew into my fabulous self. I learned that a smile got me further than tears. You know what they say—smile and the whole world smiles with you. Life was very different for me from the moment my parents realized I could charm connections they wanted to make." Easton fell silent. Nico swore he could feel the resentment seeping from Easton's pores. He made a dismissive gesture. "That's enough of that. What about you? Were you always this quiet?"

Since Nico recognized he wouldn't get more from Easton without giving a part of himself too, he answered, "Ja. I am oldest of seven, so it was be quiet or lose my voice."

"Seven? Wow. I can't imagine having six siblings. That must have been amazing."

Nico chuckled at Easton's words. Easton immediately turned his head and pressed his ear to Nico's chest, as if pressing closer to the sound. The move left Nico staring into the sexy green eyes that captured him so long ago. "You must have a good brother."

Easton smiled. It lit his eyes. "I do."

"I don't," Nico said just as fast. He hated watching Easton's smile fall, but he kept going. Easton wanted pieces of him. Nico would give them. "My papa was never home. My mama was very tired all the time. Sometimes, I felt like a parent. Never a child. I had to work from a very young age to help support the family. It was the only peace I got. I scrubbed floors and equipment at one of the best boxing schools in Germany. The owner, Otto, caught me mimicking the moves he taught others. So Otto offered to train me. There was a lot of resentment from other fighters. They paid good money to be there, being trained by the best. There I was, no better than a street urchin, stealing Otto's time."

"He must've seen something in you if he took a chance and trained you for free."

Without any plan other than to feel Easton's skin, Nico stroked Easton's cheek. Easton didn't push his hand away, so Nico didn't stop. His thumb moved across the deepest scar beneath Easton's eye. "His help wasn't free, *Knuddelbärchen*. Nothing is."

Easton took a breath. Nico felt how it shook, and he knew Easton understood. They were alike on the inside—scarred and missing parts of their soul. "What does that mean? What you just called me, that is."

A smile touched Nico's lips. "Cuddle bear."

Easton's smile made the confession worthwhile. "I don't know who told you that you should try my bakery, but I'm glad they did. It's been a really long time since I had this nice of a night." He pulled an adorable face. "Or day, for that matter," he added with a chuckle.

"We should do this again."

Easton's face brightened. "Okay."

Nico rolled upward and snagged Easton, easily pulling the man into his arms. He settled onto his back again with Easton curled against his side. He didn't press his attentions any other way. Instead, he kept his gaze locked on the sky. "So, which of these stars is the brightest? Tonight, you return to wishing."

To Nico's delight, Easton settled deeper into his hold. "Hmmm, that one," he said, pointing to the left after a moment of searching.

Nico followed the line of Easton's arm and spotted one that looked a bit brighter than the rest. "Agreed. Now, what's your wish?" Silence filled the air. Nico turned his head. Easton's face was inches from him. His eyes were closed. "If you don't say it, how can I make it true?"

A shy smile crossed Easton's lips before his eyes opened. He didn't back away. "The stars grant the wishes."

"You said they are bad at their job. Now it's Nico's job."

"I wished you'd keep showing up."

Nico kept his features blank. He didn't want Easton to see how his words moved him and run.

"That was already my plan. You should wish for something for yourself."

The way Easton bit his lip made Nico wonder if he fought a laugh. "That was a wish for me."

"Fine." Nico turned his face toward the sky and closed his eyes. "I will wish for you." A loud sigh came from Easton's chest. Nico felt its vibration against his side. "There," Nico said, turning back Easton's way.

"What did you wish for?"

"You will know when it happens."

Easton shook his head, rolled his eyes, and went back to staring at the sky. Nico didn't. There was no way Easton didn't know Nico watched him. Nico knew he had to be making the man uncomfortable. Still, Nico couldn't stop. He'd honestly never thought he'd be here. Maybe he never would be again. It was possible Easton would wake up tomorrow and remember they'd once met and where. When. How. When that moment came, they'd likely never speak again. Until then, Nico planned to bring Easton back to life. Maybe, just maybe, Easton would stick around for him. In spite of it all. There was hope.

Something buzzed. Easton jumped and dug his phone out. He checked the face and clicked around before setting the device aside and settling back down next to Nico.

"My brother. His security app didn't alert him I'd come home, and he was worried. I think this is the latest I've stayed out in over a year."

"Your brother has an app that tells him when you get home?"

Easton cut his eyes at him and laughed. "No. The house has an alarm. It alerts his phone when I've come through the door. We live together," he explained. Easton bit his lip, looking guilty. "Well, really, I live with him and his husband. They took me in last year when I was released from the hospital. After all this," he said, absently motioning toward his face. Easton never elaborated past saying he was hospitalized and motioning toward his scars. He didn't this time either. "Anyhow, Jake and Flynn are in New Orleans right now. They worry when I'm alone. He'll be fine now that he knows I'm okay."

Nico toyed with Easton's hair. "Sounds like a good brother."

"He is. Jake is almost two years younger than me, but he's better than I am." Easton's words left Nico confused, but he didn't get the chance to dig. Easton rolled to his side, facing Nico. "What about your siblings? Are they all brothers or do you have sisters too? Do they all live here or in Germany?"

Nico let Easton turn the conversation his way. He wanted Easton to know him, so he didn't evade Easton's questions. "Five sisters and one brother. The girls all have husbands and kids. They are in Germany, so I don't see them often. In fact, I have four nieces and nephews I have not met at all. It's a big bunch."

"Wait," Easton said, looking shocked, and making Nico worry their time was up. "If you're the oldest of seven and they're all old enough to be married, how old are you?"

A wave of relief washed over Nico. Easton had jumped to safer topics. "Forty-three."

"Shut up." Easton lightly smacked his chest. Nico grabbed his hand and held it there. Easton didn't seem to notice. "You don't look a day over thirty. No way in hell I would've guessed forty-three."

"It is your turn."

Easton's nose curled in the adorable way Nico couldn't resist. "I'll be thirty next Friday."

"Thirty is big. I will make it a special birthday."

Even though Easton shook his head, he didn't stop smiling. He put his head on Nico's chest, and—

like that—Nico knew he wouldn't stop. He would do whatever it took to make Easton's birthday the best damn day of his life, but it wouldn't end there. He would do everything within his power to make Easton's entire life one big wish come true. Not only did Easton deserve all the happiness in the world, Nico owed it to him. After all, it was Nico's fault he'd stopped living in the first place.

EASTON SQUEEZED THE PLUSH BEAR NICO WON him to his chest, while staring at the dark, blank wall in his bedroom. He saw nothing but the images inside his head. The way Nico had stood close when he dropped Easton at his car, making Easton wonder if he would kiss him, wouldn't budge from his brain. Nico had stroked Easton's bottom lip. He'd looked at Easton in a way Easton couldn't describe. Hungry. Easton touched his lips. Did he want Nico to kiss him? The air left Easton's lungs in a short pant. He didn't know what he wanted. They were so different. Yet, they weren't. Nico wasn't anything like the people Easton dated in the past. Maybe that was the problem. He'd never been happy. Not once. Life was always lacking something. He'd always felt disconnected. Opening his bakery was the only time he'd felt a spark for life. Before then, he'd been going through the motions, hoping something would make him feel anything at all.

This was different. Easton's stomach felt weird—like he was restless. He hadn't wanted to come home. At first, he'd chalked it up to not wanting to be alone. With Jake and Flynn gone, the place was empty, silent, and scary. Every tiny creak woke him. Now that he was here, he saw the truth. Easton hadn't wanted to leave Nico. He hadn't wanted the night to end. The carnival. The stars. None of that was him, but he'd loved every minute. The memory of Nico staring down at him, after dropping Easton at his car, flashed through Easton's mind again. Another nervous flutter tickled his gut. Easton rolled to his back and stared at the ceiling. Were they more than friends? Maybe Nico didn't see him that way at all. It was possible Nico was just a physical person. Maybe he touched everyone all the time and Easton only imagined the heated looks Nico gave. Easton lost his breath. His chest hurt at the thought. Fuck. He couldn't lie to himself. He was disappointed Nico hadn't kissed him. Easton was equally terrified at the idea of being kissed again. A growl vibrated in his throat. Why was he like this? Had that one night fucked him up this much? Or had he always been this way?

Easton tried going through the list of ways his counselor taught him on how to sort through his feelings. Nothing helped. He needed to know what Nico's intentions were. If they were only friends, that was fine. He could stamp out his desire before it grew, and he would be fine. If they were more, Easton needed to decide if he could handle it.

He closed his eyes, trying to force his mind blank. Easton caught himself trying to bury his head deeper in his pillow. He already missed Nico's chest. The steady heartbeat against his ear. With another growl, Easton sat up and snagged his phone. Sleep wasn't coming. He may as well surf the web or play a game. Any mindless thing was better than this torture.

Easton settled back down and opened his browser. He chewed his bottom lip as he stared at the blank search bar. While swallowing an odd pang of guilt, Easton typed Nico's name. His verified pages showed up first, followed by page after page, recapping the titles he'd held and fights he'd won. His garage didn't show up until Easton was six pages deep. Easton switched to images. He scrolled and scrolled until he hit an image of a nude Nico. Only a small white towel, covering his junk, kept Easton from enjoying the entire picture. Without an ounce of shame, he held his finger on the image until his phone gave him the option to save it. He eyed Nico's large, hard muscles. When Easton had touched Nico, Nico's body felt beneath Easton's hands the way it looked under his clothes. Easton caught himself running his finger down the image, wishing the towel wasn't blocking his view. A text message popped up, covering Nico's face, and startling a sound from Easton he couldn't describe. Heat exploded across his face. It was Nico. Easton laughed. Even to his ears, it sounded horrified. It was like Nico knew Easton had been drooling over his body. He opened the message.

Nico: *You're probably sleeping, but I can't.*

A huge smile pulled at Easton's lips. He shouldn't read too much into things, but he quickly responded.

Easton: *I can't either.*

Nico: *What are you doing?*

Another laugh escaped Easton. He toyed with the bear and tried to think of something to say that wouldn't make him look like an idiot.

Easton: *I just searched your name online.*

He hit send, dropped the phone, and covered his

face with both hands. Peals of horrified laughter shook him. Why had he done that? He was so stupid. The phone vibrated. Easton took a breath and checked the message.

Nico: *Find anything good?*

Fuck it.

Easton: *There are some interesting images of you online.*

Nico: *Oh. You must've landed on the photo shoot I did for that skin magazine. It was a bit humiliating, but they paid me a lot of money. A lot.*

There were full nudes out there somewhere? He was so searching for those later.

Easton: *Nooooo. LOL! I didn't see those. Kinda disappointed now.*

Even as he sent the message, he couldn't stop laughing. This was nuts. The phone rang in his hand. Easton covered his eyes and let it ring twice more before deciding to answer.

"Hello?" Yeah, that was his squeaky voice. He cleared his throat and tried again. "Hello?"

"I could send them to you."

Fuck. That deep voice and accent. Easton took a breath. He really wanted those pics. "You don't have to do that." Nico might want something in exchange and that wasn't happening.

"Do you want them?"

God help him. He couldn't say no, but Easton also couldn't force his lips to say yes.

"I didn't mean to make you uncomfortable."

Nico's claim shook Easton's voice loose. "I'm not uncomfortable. Send them." He covered his eyes again. Yep. That just happened. His phone shook with incoming messages. With his heart in his throat, he switched to speaker phone and opened the first one. Easton nearly choked on his tongue. Nico was more than nude. He was hard and his face was flushed with arousal. Easton's body tingled as he scrolled through each one. Nico was huge in every way and beautiful. Easton had never been attracted to big, bulky men with tattoos. There was something about Nico, though. Easton fought the urge to lick his phone.

"Your silence is deafening." Nico truly sounded nervous—like he might've made a mistake.

Easton cleared his throat. "I'm speechless. These are really good." Easton picked through his words, trying not to sound as thirsty as he felt. "I'm feeling a bit inferior." He unwillingly tacked on with a nervous chuckle.

"Why inferior?"

He rolled his eyes. Nico wasn't blind. Easton

didn't understand why he pretended not to know Easton looked like he'd been nearly carved to pieces, because that was exactly what had happened to him. Rather than saying that, as he should, Easton lied. "I'm a little guy. You must've worked out since the day you were born."

"You're perfect." A snort escaped Easton before he could stop it. "You are," Nico said, sounding on the edge of anger. His rage had Easton's mind going blank. Nico continued and Easton hung on every word. "I want to touch you way more than I do, but I hold back, because I don't think you look at me the same way. When I dropped you off tonight, I almost took a chance and kissed you. I lost my nerve. If you want to only be friends, that's what we'll do. You can forget all this. I will too."

Easton's heart raced. His chest rose and fell at a rapid pace. He didn't want Nico to forget this. "I like you." Easton didn't think he was making himself clear, but he was terrified.

"Okay." Nico sounded confused.

Easton forced himself to try harder. "As more than a friend."

"Oh." That was better. Nico sounded a little better.

Easton wanted even more. "I wish you'd kissed

me." He had to be honest, though. "But I'm a bit of a mess. I can't promise how I'll react. No one's kissed me since... I'd like to try," Easton said louder than he intended. He took a breath and clutched the bear to his chest.

"We'll work on it together. I will keep you safe."

Easton fought a smile. Nico was so strong and sure of his abilities. Easton was every bit the mess he claimed to be and would probably fail. "I'm not working tomorrow."

"Text me your address. We will spend the day together."

"Okay."

"For now, you will talk to me until you get tired."

Easton stared into the darkness. He didn't think Nico meant to sound so bossy, but it was oddly comforting. "I'd like that."

"Tell me about all your favorite things."

"Only if you agree to do the same." Because Easton needed to know those things like he needed his next breath.

Nico didn't hesitate. "Of course, *Knuddelbärchen*. Whatever pleases you."

A soft laugh came out breathless. "I like that. What you call me," Easton said, clarifying. "It kind of makes me feel warm all over."

"Good. That's just how I want you."

Easton couldn't stop smiling or hugging the bear Nico won. He was ridiculously happy, and it was addicting. Even though he didn't know what tomorrow would bring, maybe he'd flip if Nico kissed him, but Easton wanted to try living again. He'd never expected that would happen. Nico had something special. Easton wanted more.

FOUR

IT WASN'T unusual for Nico to run on a few hours of sleep. Today, his impatience to see Easton had him moving on even fewer hours. The house where Easton stayed was in one of the poshest neighborhoods around. Nico had toured a few houses on this street when looking to buy his own home. In the end, he'd chosen to build a place where he wouldn't have neighbors and plenty of room for his car collection.

When Easton answered, Nico fought the urge to throw the man over his shoulder and find the nearest flat surface. He looked sexy as fuck in his white jeans and a light green shirt. Unfortunately, for Nico's plans, the outfit wouldn't work.

Easton looked shy for some reason. "Hi."

"You are beautiful. Where's your bedroom?"

At Nico's question, Easton blinked. "What?"

"We need to find clothes you won't ruin."

"Excuse me?"

Nico took Easton's hand and brought it to his lips. He kissed it while holding Easton's stare. "Bedroom. Where is it?"

Without another word, Easton led Nico through the living room and down the hall. His booted footsteps sounded loud on the marble floors. Everything he passed was pristine and expensive. The wood shined and smelled like furniture cleaner. Nico didn't spare a glance for much other than Easton. His ass looked delectable in his form-fitting jeans. Easton's hair was perfectly styled, and Nico wanted to make a mess of him. The fifth door they came to, Easton stepped inside, towing Nico along behind him. As soon as he cleared the threshold, Nico knew he could've picked Easton's room out by himself. The sun shone bright, lighting every corner. Everything was light-colored and fluffy. His bed looked soft. The comforter gave Nico the impression he'd sink into it and disappear—like a fluffy cloud. The rainbow-colored bear sat in the center of the bed—like he'd slept with Easton. Nico couldn't stop looking in every direction, learning everything there was to know about Easton. Hair care products, cologne, and what looked to be a million other bottles were scattered on his white dresser.

"I didn't know what you had planned today, so I didn't know how to dress."

Nico shook off the spell of Easton's too-cheery bedroom. "Let's find you something you don't mind ruining."

"How do you mean? Will it be ruined beyond being worn again or just dark-colored because we'll be in the dirt?"

"The first."

Easton cast a look around the room while chewing on his bottom lip as if he didn't own a single thing that fit the bill. "Um..."

"Let's look together," Nico offered. "Dresser or closet?"

"Closet," Easton said with a nod, as if getting onboard.

Nico moved to the closet and opened the door. The closet turned out to be almost as big as the bedroom. It was stuffed full of clothes, shoes, and even a few unpacked boxes. Nico pulled out the first dark-colored item he spotted. It was a black V-neck t-shirt. "This will do," he said more for himself than

Easton. Next, he found some dark jeans. He turned Easton's way. "Put these on."

Easton looked uncomfortable. He didn't move to take the clothes from Nico. "Okay." Even though Easton agreed, he didn't budge.

Nico crossed the room and snagged the hem of Easton's shirt. He knew exactly what the problem was, and Nico wasn't having it. While holding Easton's stare, his lifted the material.

Easton flew into full-blown panic mode. He fought Nico for the shirt. "I'll stay home."

"Stop." Nico didn't raise his voice. He kept his tone level. "Easton, stop."

The fire drained from Easton, but so too did the life. His shoulders sagged. Easton's gaze dropped to the floor. "Whatever."

It wasn't Nico's intention to break him. Nico needed Easton to see he wasn't his scars. He touched Easton's chin, forcing Easton's gaze back to his. Light green irises focused on Nico. Nico shuffled closer and dipped his chin. Easton leaned away a hair. Nico chased him. Their lips touched. For a moment, Easton stood frozen beneath Nico's lips. Then, his lips parted. He lightly sucked Nico's bottom lip. His tongue swiped Nico's lip. Nico let him lead. He opened for Easton. Their tongues met. Passion exploded through their kiss. As their tongues played, Nico used the opportunity to push Easton's shirt higher. He counted Easton's ribs with his thumbs as he drew the material upward. Nico pulled away and swept the shirt up and over Easton's head. He reclaimed Easton's mouth before Easton had time to panic again. Nico flattened his palms against Easton's back and urged him closer. He memorized the bumps of Easton's spine as he headed south. Easton didn't protest. Nico took advantage. Easton's ass filled his hands. Nico squeezed, going hard with the perfect, firm globes beneath his fingers.

Nico kissed a path from Easton's mouth to his ear. He lightly nipped at Easton's ear lobe. "You're fucking beautiful. Please don't hide from me."

"I'm trying." Easton's response sounded winded.

"I know, *Knuddelbärchen*. In this, I ask you to trust me. Keep your eyes on me." Nico pulled away long enough to grab the dark-colored shirt he'd picked out. He dressed Easton as he would a child. Easton tolerated Nico's ministrations, but he looked wrecked—like he knew Nico would walk away now. Nico crowded Easton's space again. He led Easton's hand to his erection. "I want you. Call me a liar." He held Easton's gaze, daring Easton with his stare to say the words. Nico released Easton's hand, giving him the freedom to do as he pleased. Easton didn't treat him the way Nico had come to expect from everyone else. Nico was famous in certain circles. He'd never had a problem finding someone to fuck. Nico didn't want just anyone. He wanted Easton. But Easton took a step back. A line appeared between his eyebrows. He looked confused. Nico had a bad feeling they were backsliding.

Nico couldn't take it. "Talk to me."

Easton focused on him. "Is it okay if we kiss again?"

Hunger roared inside Nico. He closed the gap between them and claimed Easton's mouth. He wasn't gentle. Nico poured every ounce of longing into their kiss. Easton didn't realize how far above Nico he was. Nico had come from the streets. Everything he had, he'd literally fought for. Easton deserved someone soft. Nico was hard inside and out, but there was something about Easton.

Easton clung to his chest. His kisses were sweet, making Nico's chest feel tight. It wasn't sexual. Their kiss was a connection made. A silent promise made by touch. Easton was the first to break their kiss, but he didn't pull away. With two handfuls of Nico's shirt held tightly in his fists, Easton pressed his forehead to Nico's chest.

Nico rubbed Easton's back. He soaked up the way Easton clung to him. The moment gave him hope. Still, Easton's silence scared him a little. "Are you still with me?"

Easton nodded, squishing his forehead against Nico's chest with every move he made. "I'm just guilty of being the cuddler you accuse me of being. You're big and cozy. I don't want to move. Nobody holds me anymore, and I don't sleep."

A bark of laughter escaped Nico. "My ego might never recover. I'm putting you to sleep."

"Your ego has nothing to worry about." Easton kissed his sternum. "You're beautiful and wanted. I guess I should finish changing."

Nico held his tongue and kept his hands to himself. While Easton stripped off his pants, Nico moved to the window under the guise of giving Easton privacy. Instead, he pulled the curtains closed. He moved to the other window and did the same. Nico moved quickly. He didn't want to give Easton time to put on his jeans.

A chuckle sounded behind him. "Do you have something against the sun?"

"It's harder to sleep in a bright room." Nico turned. Easton held his jeans, looking confused. "You won't need those."

Easton's open confusion turned to worry. He chewed his bottom lip, looking like he didn't know if he should ask.

Nico nodded toward the bed. "Get in."

Easton's gaze slid toward the bed. He didn't stop worrying at his bottom lip. With a sigh, Nico walked over and turned down the covers. He didn't look at Easton as he kicked off his shoes. From the corner of his eye, Nico saw Easton move. He eased into bed in slow increments—like he still considered bolting. Nico didn't rush. He wasn't trying to frighten Easton. Nico waited until he was climbing into the bed to look at Easton again. Easton was wide eyed and looked scared as hell. Nico's heart squeezed in his chest.

"It's okay, *Knuddelbärchen*. My plans for the day can wait. It's your day off and you should sleep. I will hold you."

Easton cleared his throat. "In your jeans?"

Nico bit back a smile. "You are nervous. This is fine."

He settled on his side and tugged Easton into his arms. Easton didn't argue, but he also didn't relax. His every muscle remained stiff. Nico imagined that his erection digging into Easton's ass didn't help matters, but Nico couldn't help it. It was Easton in his arms and his body knew it. Easton's muscles slowly relaxed as he realized Nico had no plans to molest him. Nico wondered if Easton even noticed that he stroked the arm Nico had draped over him. It was all Nico could focus on. He caught himself kissing Easton's hair for the fourth time. Nico closed his eyes and forced his mind clear. Easton's breathing evened and then deepened. Nico focused on the sound. Everything was as it should be. Nico was there, between the door and Easton, holding the man he'd fallen in love with from a distance. Nico didn't doubt for a second the rest of the world would think he was crazy. Maybe he was, but he currently held the center of his obsession. Nothing else mattered to him.

A STEADY HEARTBEAT THUMPED BENEATH Easton's ear. He was so warm and comfy. A familiar scent penetrated his brain. Awareness slowly seeped in. His eyes opened. The room was dark. Easton took another deep breath, soaking up the delicious scent. He shifted slightly before deciding he was too comfy to move. The realization that he was draped over Nico like a blanket slowly dawned. Even as he came back to himself, Easton couldn't convince himself to move. As solid as Nico was, Easton couldn't believe the guy was the softest mattress in the world. Easton's muscles were useless.

Nico shifted in his sleep. He grabbed Easton's ass and pulled him higher—like he snuggled deeper beneath the covers. Easton stifled a laugh. The move left him with his face buried in the crook of Nico's neck. Easton took advantage and burrowed closer. He could stay like this for the rest of his life. Easton couldn't remember ever feeling so comfortable and safe. Cherished. He could easily become addicted to this.

Nico had been hard as stone when Easton had fallen asleep. How many men would've done that for him? He'd never met anyone who didn't expect sex. Every man he'd ever dated had demanded Easton put their needs above his. Nico was different. He'd ignored his lust so Easton could sleep, and damn, Easton felt good for the first time in forever. He didn't know what time it was, but he'd slept solid. No nightmares had come for him. Without thought, Easton kissed Nico's neck. Once his lips were pressed against Nico's skin, Easton found his lips parting. He needed to know how Nico's skin tasted.

Nico's hands slid across his back. His arms

tightened around Easton. "How did you sleep, sexy?"

Easton smiled against Nico's skin. His deep voice was twice as rough while sleep still clung to his vocal chords. "Solid," Easton answered with a soft chuckle. He wasn't ready to move. "No nightmares or anything."

The hands rubbing his back fell still. "Do you have a lot of nightmares?"

For a moment, Easton debated lying. He was already nodding before he decided to be honest. It was Nico. Something about him made it impossible for Easton to hide.

"You will sleep with me from now on. Nico will keep you safe."

A burst of surprised laughter escaped Easton. Nico was so fucking outrageous and sure of himself. "You have a life. I don't expect you to do this all time." Damned if Nico hadn't kept him safe from even his dreams, though. It was ridiculous for one person to be so much of everything.

"You didn't ask. I didn't offer. This is how things will be. You need sleep."

Easton could argue. He knew there were things he should probably say. Instead, he kept snuggling. Whatever happened would happen. If Easton knew nothing else, he knew he didn't have control over anything at all. "What did you have planned for today that we missed?"

Nico's hands slipped beneath Easton's shirt. He rubbed Easton's back skin on skin. "Nothing that can't wait. I planned to take you to work with me and let you tinker with the Mustang."

Guilt washed over Easton. "I made you miss work? Now I feel terrible."

Without warning, Nico shoved his hands down the back of Easton's underwear. He massaged the globes of Easton's ass and Easton's mind went blank. His dick went hard. Then the terror struck, side-swiping him. Easton scrambled from the bed, stumbling and uncaring of how he looked as he made a break for the bathroom. Once there, he flipped on the lights and caught sight of himself in the mirror. His face was flushed, and his hair was a mess. Inside, he was a car wreck with maximum casualties. It was like an interstate pile up in there. Easton didn't know if he'd ever be whole again. He felt sick. What if Nico left? Surely, now he realized Easton was a waste of his time, and he'd disappear. The thought alone was heartbreaking. Easton didn't want to be this person. He missed being the cutesy charmer. This was bullshit.

Nico appeared in the doorway. Easton couldn't make himself meet Nico's stare. Nico moved slow, slipping inside the bathroom and pressing against Easton's back. Easton watched their reflections. Something about seeing things happen through the mirror made them less real—like watching a movie. Nico kissed his shoulder.

"You don't have to be scared, *Knuddelbärchen*. I want you, but I can control myself." Nico's lips brushed Easton's shoulder several times during his claim. Easton couldn't recall experiencing this much lust with anyone else. In truth, sex had been pretty meh for him over the years. It was one of those things he hadn't thought much about other than pleasing whoever took care of him at the time. Then, in a dark van between the pain and the fear, this part of him had been stolen along with his beauty. In fact, all the gorgeous things in life had been ripped away from him, so that even when he looked in the mirror, nothing normal was left behind. Now here was Nico, giving pieces of Easton back. He wanted to lie and say he wasn't afraid. When he tried, his teeth chattered, forcing him to lock his back teeth together.

Nico straightened and set his chin on Easton's head. It really was ridiculous how much taller Nico was than him. Easton was used to being short, but this was nuts. He stared at their reflection. Damn. They looked good together, though. It was like Easton fit just perfectly against him. Easton smiled. He was definitely the little spoon.

"You are beautiful, yes?"

Easton held Nico's stare in the mirror. He smirked. "That's not what I was thinking. We look like we fit."

A huge puppy-dog grin stretched Nico's face. He nodded, digging his chin into Easton's head with each bob. Easton laughed but cringed, trying to get away. Nico's laugh kept him from running away. Everything should be uncomfortable, and Nico should be making his way for the hills after Easton's earlier reaction. Instead, he was playing with Easton and being a big kid. Something grew inside Easton's chest. The only person to stick by him no matter how hard Easton made things was his brother, Jake. Now, here this guy was, being fucking perfect. Easton's eyes stung. He didn't want to lose this.

"I need a shower."

Nico gave him one more squeeze. "Okay." He started to pull away.

Easton held on to Nico's arms. "Stay." Even though he wasn't sure how much he could handle,

Easton wanted to try. Here in the light where he could see who he touched.

For a moment, Nico held his stare. Finally, he nodded. "Anytime you want me to go, I will."

With a dip of his chin, Easton dropped his gaze and moved to the shower. It had taken him a few tries, when he first moved in, to figure out the shower. It had so many buttons and switches, Easton needed a damn owner's manual to figure things out. Now he knew the combo of three switches to create the perfect shower. He turned to find Nico watching him. Nico looked so goddamn delicious. It didn't matter Nico wasn't Easton's usual type. Nico was universally sexy. Tall, chiseled, and confident. With his shirt missing and his jeans unbuttoned, Nico looked like a sexy god. The hunger he tried to hide had Easton feeling exposed and excited all at once. The line of his thick erection in his jeans drew Easton's eye. He tried looking away.

"Get in," Nico said, nodding toward the shower. "I'll give you a second to breathe."

Easton pushed his underwear down his hips. There was no hiding the fact that he wanted Nico, especially once he peeled off his shirt, leaving himself completely exposed. Easton tried to move slow to hide his nervousness. He stepped inside the shower and immediately ducked beneath the water to hide his hot cheeks. Jesus. He didn't know what was wrong with him. Easton didn't used to be this way. Being shy and skittish wasn't his nature. If anything, he'd been efficient—gotten the job done with minimal fuss. Easton let that sink in. In truth, he'd probably been a bit bland in bed. Before Nico, he hadn't cared if things were boring. Now Easton wished he was the opposite of everything he'd always been.

The shower door opened, and Nico stepped in. Those smoking hot photos he'd dropped on Easton last night now came to life. Easton couldn't tear his eyes away. Nico was very... manly. In every way.

Without thought, Easton reached for Nico. Their bodies collided. Easton's knees nearly buckled when Nico's cock hit him in the stomach. He was too turned on to panic. The rain shower above them made it hard for Easton to meet Nico's stare without drowning. That left one direction to look. Easton couldn't stare directly at Nico's dick and not touch it. At least, that was what he told himself as his fingers closed around the gigantic cock between them. Easton had an overwhelming urge to put it in his mouth. He couldn't explain it. The roof of his mouth itched with anticipation. He was forced to swallow all the saliva filling his mouth. Easton knew he couldn't just stand there, holding it all day. Nico wasn't moving or saying a word. Easton stood there, holding the guy's dick and staring down at it while trying to decide if he had the nerve to lick it.

"This is... *argh*." Whatever Nico intended to say ended in a jumbled cry as Easton found his courage, bent, and jumped in with both feet. He took Nico to the back of his throat without preamble. It was too late to turn back now. Nico tasted every bit as satisfying as Easton suspected he would. Salty pre-cum filled his mouth. Easton hummed in delight. A strangled sound came from Nico. Easton was disconnected from everything except what he wanted. In a detached way, he knew Nico touched everywhere he could reach. Easton's entire being was focused on his feast. He licked and sucked. If anyone had ever tasted so good, Easton couldn't recall a time. He wanted more of the salt. He sucked harder, determined to have it. The sounds coming from Nico got louder. Easton knew he was close to getting what he sought. His anticipation grew by the second along with his lust. Easton ignored everything but the dick in his mouth. He used both hands and his throat to chase the cum he needed. Nico stiffened. A flood of hot cum filled Easton's mouth. A happy hum escaped him as he licked it away. He chased every drop, wiggling his tongue all over Nico's cock until Nico begged for mercy. Nico urged him upright and tucked Easton against his chest. He could hear Nico's ragged breathing and racing heart. Easton smiled at the sound. For the first time in a long time, he was at peace.

Before his head left the clouds, Nico swept him off his feet and set him on the bench built into the wall. With one hand lightly holding Easton's jaw, Nico kept Easton's gaze locked on him as his other hand massaged Easton's erection. Easton knew it wouldn't take much. Sucking Nico's dick had brought him to the edge. Pressure already beat at his crown. Nico's intense stare had Easton clinging to the edge of the bench to stay grounded. He'd never seen so much passion directed at him. They hadn't kissed. The moment seemed more powerful because kisses were missing. They were focused on each other's pleasure. Not their own. Easton barely blinked. The determination in Nico's stare was arresting. He wanted Easton's orgasm every bit as much as Easton had wanted his. Easton pressed his back against the wall and fought to reach explosion. He was so close. Nico's motions quickened. Easton sucked air, fighting to breathe as he reached the cliff.

A cry tore from his throat. The orgasm rocked him to his core as it hit. Nico never once looked away. He kept pumping until Easton almost begged him to stop. Then, Nico moved closer. He towed Easton's hips forward until he had no choice but to wrap his legs around Nico's hips. Their bodies touched in the most intimate way. It took Easton's already ragged breath.

"See how brave you are?"

A tired-sounding chuckle escaped Easton. Bravery had nothing to do with it. "See how hot you make me?"

A smile exploded across Nico's face. "I'm seeing a lot of things—like how we were meant to meet."

Yeah. Easton saw that too. It was beautiful.

FIVE

NICO: *Knuddelbärchen.*

    Easton: *Yes?*

    Nico: *I miss you.*

    Easton: *I miss you too.*

    Nico: *Good. I will fix it.*

EASTON: *JAKE COMES HOME TONIGHT. I'M READY to see his face.*

    Nico: *Then I will let you visit with your much-missed baby brother.*

    Easton: *I miss you too, though.*

    Nico: *Come to me afterward. I will fix it.*

    Easton: *Okay.*

EVEN THOUGH NICO KNEW HE WAS TAKING A huge risk, he still pulled into the first open parking spot he saw at the bookstore connected to Easton's Bakery. Some things were too important to hide due to fear. There was every probability that Nico would cross the threshold of Baby Boy's Books and Jake or Flynn would know exactly who he was. There was no risk Nico wasn't willing to take for Easton.

As he cleared the door, Nico spotted a skinny, tall guy with dark blond hair. He was the only person working, so Nico headed his way. The man's chin lifted. The eyes that focused on Nico were Easton's eyes. They were such an exact match that Nico nearly missed a step. There wasn't a single other thing about the guy that looked like Easton, but there could be no doubt. This was Easton's brother.

Nico pasted on his friendliest smile. "Are you Jake?"

Jake nodded.

With his hand outstretched, Nico moved closer. "My name is Nico. I'm dating Easton."

Jake was reaching for Nico's hand when he hesitated. His eyebrows damn near hit his hairline. "Seriously?"

Nico's smile slipped. "Why the disbelief?"

With a shake of his head, Jake chuckled and accepted Nico's handshake. "Sorry. You're very different from anyone Easton's dated in the past."

"I'll take your compliment," Nico said with a chuckle.

Jake smiled. "Then I already like you better than anyone he's dated. He's not working today."

Nico nodded. "I know. That's why I came by. His birthday is tomorrow, and I need your help to pull off a surprise."

Mischief flashed in Jake's eyes and the resemblance grew between the brothers. "In that case, whatever you need, I'm in."

"Good." Nico needed an ally. He planned to make Easton's birthday a day he wouldn't soon forget. Nico needed all the help he could get to sneak under Easton's radar. He fully intended to spoil the man who lived beneath Nico's skin. He had a feeling the opportunities where Easton allowed Nico to give him everything would be few and far between. This was one time Nico intended to demand acquiescence. Easton's birthday would be special if it killed him. When the day came that Easton learned the truth about him and booted Nico from his life, Nico wanted Easton to have nothing but happy memories with him. Even if it cost Nico his heart. "He'll probably be angry."

"Great," Jake chirped, as if he relished the thought of someone pulling Easton from his comfort zone. Nico knew then he'd come to the right place.

EVEN THOUGH EASTON WAS TAKING MORE DAYS off since he'd started dating Nico, he still worked more than any normal person should. He'd been up since three, making a variety of baked goods. Flynn and Jake were back, but he was still alone in a too silent house since they both had left early for the bookstore. Easton had been fighting the urge to call Nico since two minutes after he'd woken up to an empty bed. He was tired and cranky. Everything sucked and even Easton didn't know why. He missed his giant too-rough-around-the-edges angel and nothing would be right again until he saw Nico again. It was ridiculous how dependent he'd become on Nico's overwhelming presence. He was a grown man who should be able to eat, bathe, and sleep without being told when and where to do those things. Yet everything felt wrong without Nico. Easton wanted to growl at his own childishness. In the past year, he'd worked so hard at becoming independent. He was, Easton reminded himself. Yet, he didn't necessarily want to be. It was a conundrum he was still learning to deal with.

The unmistakable growl of a Harley brought Easton's head up. He listened for half a beat before racing for the door. Once there, he straightened his clothes and tried to act like he hadn't just sprinted through the house like a complete lunatic. Fuck, he had it bad. Easton forced himself to wait to open the door until after the doorbell rang. In fact, he counted to ten so Nico wouldn't know he'd been impatiently waiting on the other side. The welcoming smile stretching his lips widened at the first sight of Nico. Goddamn, he was hot. His jeans fit just right in all the perfect places while his sleeveless shirt showed off his massive arms and tattoos. Easton's mouth watered. He'd never felt more shameless.

A heated glance swept down Easton's body, making him tingle. "There he is," Nico said, before tackling Easton and tossing him over his shoulder. A loud burst of laughter exploded from Easton. Nico kicked the front door closed behind him as he headed for the recliner. Easton tried to protest the manhandling, but he couldn't stop laughing. Not to mention he could barely breathe with Nico's gigantic shoulder in his stomach.

Nico let Easton's body slide down his as he reached the chair. Easton's arms automatically encircled Nico's neck. With his feet still hanging more than a foot from the floor, Nico captured Easton's mouth. Nico sat. Easton happily straddled Nico's body while their tongues played. Happiness lived in Nico's arms. His fingers found Nico's soft hair. He toyed with the locks while sucking the man's bottom lip.

Nico kissed a path to Easton's ear, then on to his neck. His fingers found the leg of Easton's shorts and slipped inside. "I've never seen you this dressed down. It's hot."

Easton tilted his head, giving Nico all the access to his throat. It was true. He'd found a pair of cutoff sweats and an old t-shirt when he'd gotten up. Several times he'd thought to change but never made it back to the bedroom. Now Easton was glad he hadn't. "If I'd known how little effort it took to make you this hot, I would've been a little lazier sooner."

Nico chuckled against his skin. "To be fair, you're always sexy. This is just a new side of you to me." He leaned away and met Easton's stare. "Did you sleep?"

Easton's gaze slid away. "A little."

"Not good enough. What have you been doing this morning?"

"Nothing." Easton dragged the word out, trying his best to sound innocent.

"*Knuddelbärchen,* what have you been doing this morning? Don't forget I can smell."

Easton chuckled. Even to his ears, it sounded nervous. "It's just cinnamon rolls."

"And?"

"A cake," Easton admitted.

"And?"

Easton chewed his bottom lip. "Scones."

"Anything else?"

His shoulders fell. "Does it matter?"

Nico was the naughtiest version of sweet that Easton had ever seen. He eyed Easton, looking like an understanding parent. "Baby, I know you love what you do. You're amazing, but between not sleeping, keeping the bakery open sixteen hours a day, and spending your days off cooking, you'll be burned out within a year. What happens then?"

Easton hadn't really thought about it. He'd just been keeping his hands busy, trying hard not to backslide into the person he used to be. "I don't know how to stop. No one but Jake really believed I could be a success. If I slow down and fail... I don't want that."

"You're not capable of failing and I don't want you to change. Just breathe occasionally, okay?"

Easton nodded. No one worried about him. It was nice. "I'm breathing right now. The rest of the day is all about you."

"It needs to be all about you," Nico said, sounding grumbly and sexy.

"Grumbly bear," Easton said, infusing as much affection as he felt in the words. "It'll be all about us."

"Good boy." Easton's mouth went dry at the praise. Nico was so much of everything no one else had ever been. The man's intense stare had Easton ready to pant. "Reach in my pocket, *Knuddelbärchen*."

Easton furrowed his brow and shuffled back a little. Even in his new position, he couldn't get his hand in Nico's jeans. Nico kicked out the footstool of the recliner, nearly toppling Easton and making him laugh. He rolled to one hip next to Nico and dipped his hand inside Nico's pants. Easton half expected this to be some sort of sexual ploy, but his fingers collided with something. He tugged. A fine gold chain with a tiny teddy bear charm filled his palm.

Easton stared down at it in silence. Nico took it from Easton and undid the clasp. He put it around Easton's neck. It fell perfectly over his collarbone. Easton was speechless. It wasn't that it was a massively expensive gift. That wasn't what moved him. It was that it was the perfect gift.

Easton couldn't look away from Nico as Nico brushed his fingertips down the line of the necklace. "There. You can think of your cranky bear every time you see it."

"It's beautiful." Even to Easton's ears, he sounded moved.

Nico's hand lingered on Easton's chest. "You make it that way." Nico made him feel. Easton didn't know the words to explain everything crowding his brain. Nico overwhelmed him, making Easton want to be worthy of the way Nico treated him. He'd never felt this way before. Easton would find a way to be worthy of him.

WITH EASTON SLEEPING PEACEFULLY ON NICO'S chest, Nico was in heaven. Easton's every breath caressed his neck. His heartbeat kissed Nico's chest. Nico's eyes kept falling closed, even though he wasn't the least bit tired. He was savoring every second. For over a year, he'd watched Easton. Easton was his secret. He was that one hidden longing no one knew about. A coveted dream Nico never expected would be his. Nico knew it wasn't right for him to be in Easton's life. He knew no one would understand. Maybe Easton was a sickness. Nico comforted himself with the knowledge that he would spoil Easton. He would never let him be scared or unhappy. Nico wouldn't expect or ask for more than Easton could give. Maybe Nico was wrong, but Easton wouldn't suffer for Nico's insanity.

Easton shifted in his sleep. His hand slipped beneath Nico's shirt. Nico pulled the covers higher in case Easton was cold. He went back to savoring every sensation of having Easton in his arms. Once Easton had a nap and was caught up on the sleep he'd missed last night, Nico would take him to dinner. Maybe they'd go for a ride down the ocean highway and get some fresh air. Easton shifted again. This time, his hand moved lower, coming to rest on Nico's cock. Nico sucked in a breath. They still hadn't made love. Nico was cool with that. He wouldn't rush Easton after the hell he'd suffered. Damned if Easton didn't keep him hard, though. He hadn't stopped thinking about that shower blow job since it happened. Vanity aside, he'd spent a lot of time as a heavyweight champion and benefited sexually from that title way more than any man should. Even with having lived through all that, no one had ever blown him the way Easton had. It hadn't been about Nico. Easton had licked and sucked Nico for his own pleasure and it had been the most mind-blowing experience in his life. His dick was hard thinking about it. Easton's hand on it didn't help.

Nico drew a deep breath through his nose and let it out slowly. He stared at the ceiling of Easton's bedroom and tried to clear his mind. Warm lips brushed his throat. His eyes fell closed. Damn. He'd definitely have blue balls later. Easton shifted higher and kissed Nico's neck again. He stifled a groan as his cock jumped. Easton popped the button on Nico's jeans. His tongue tickled Nico's skin. Nico was tap dancing on hope, trying to squash it before it became an inferno. His zipper came down one tooth at a time. Nico ground his back teeth to a pulp. Easton pushed Nico's jeans and underwear down one hip. Nico lifted, letting him have them. Easton took advantage and worked them down the other. Even still, Nico refused to get it in his head that this would go anywhere. He'd taken off his shirt before they'd gotten in bed. Easton took advantage of that too by slipping lower and scraping Nico's nipple with his teeth. Nico stayed still, letting Easton do as much or as little as he wanted. He wouldn't pressure Easton either way. But it was getting harder not to hope as his clothes disappeared and Easton shimmied out of his too.

When Easton's fingertips brushed the length of Nico's erection, he swallowed a moan. He was scared shitless if he made a single sound Easton would stop. Easton's touch disappeared. Nico squeezed his eyes shut, fighting his body. His eyes flew open again when he heard plastic crinkle. Easton rolled a condom down Nico's length. With his head bent over his task, Nico couldn't see Easton's expression. He dropped his head and closed his eyes again. Nico got the feeling Easton felt freer when Nico wasn't watching. Easton's mouth opened over Nico's ribs, making him squirm. A soft chuckle vibrated against his skin. That one tiny sound made him hotter than all the touches that came before it. Easton kissed his way up Nico's body, straddling his hips. Their lips met. Nico's head automatically left the pillow trying to get closer. Easton placed light kisses at the corner of Nico's mouth as he positioned Nico's erection. Nico held his breath. The air left his lungs in one loud breath as Easton took him inside. He almost blew right then. The combination of wanting Easton so long and Easton's tight heat punched Nico hard. Thankfully, Easton moved slow. Nico caught his breath. His hands landed on Easton's hips. He prayed touching Easton wouldn't make him stop, but Nico wanted Easton to enjoy the ride. Nico led Easton into a different angle, ensuring each thrust massaged the perfect spot. A ragged-sounding whimper filled the air, letting Nico know he'd succeeded. Nico watched Easton ride him, treating the moment like the fantasy come to life it was. He wanted to remember everything. Easton was so goddamn strong and brave. Nico didn't think Easton realized it, but Nico saw.

Their motions never turned frantic. Instead, their lovemaking was slow, hot, and soul-shaking. Easton's light green gaze latched on to Nico. Nico was transfixed. A flush rode high on Easton's cheeks, making his eyes seem even lighter. His lips were slightly parted. Nico knew he was close. He reached between them and stroked, helping Easton along. Nico needed Easton to get there because he was ready to blow. There was no warning. The sexiest sound Nico had ever heard slipped from Easton. His body convulsed, sucking Nico's cock deep and making his vision dim. Hot cum coated Nico's body while his mind flew apart. The spring that had been winding tighter finally broke, shaking him to his core. An orgasm rocked his body while love totally fucked his mind. He'd already been obsessed to the point of unhealthy with Easton. As he hauled Easton down for a kiss, Nico found a new depth of insanity. Easton was his. Nico would die for him. After all, dying was nothing. Nico had already done worse things for Easton.

SIX

THE SUN WAS BRIGHT, and birds were chirping. It was a beautiful day to turn thirty. Easton pulled a face, even though there was no one to see him. He gathered the boxes of muffins he'd made for the nurses and headed for the door. To some, thirty might be a special number. Hell, to most, any birthday was a special day. For Easton, it was just another day. He couldn't lie and say it wasn't a bit depressing. Easton never wanted to leave his twenties. There had been plenty of times he'd wished for a huge party where everyone celebrated him. Who wouldn't want that? Despite his many charms, Easton wasn't good at making friends. There was no one who would come to a party for him, much less throw one for him.

Before Easton made it to the door, his phone rang. He growled as he dumped the boxes he'd just picked up back on the counter.

Easton dug out his phone. "Hello?"

"Happy birthday!"

A smile exploded across Easton's face at the sound of his nephew's voice. Technically, Trace was Flynn's son and only Easton's nephew by marriage, but Easton took being an uncle seriously. Trace was —most likely—the only nephew Easton would ever have. "Hey, sweetie. Thank you. How have you been?" Easton swore he could hear the charm in Trace's voice when he spoke. He was twenty-one and gorgeous. Everyone loved him, of course. Trace was perfect. He could sweet talk the birds from the trees.

"I'm good. Tell me about your day so far. Have you gotten tons of presents? Are you tired of hearing the phone ring?"

"Not everyone can be popular like you. No presents and you're the first person to call. How are things in Colorado? Oooh, how's that sexy husband?"

"Good on all counts. What do you mean no presents? What kind of shit show is my dad running around there? If I was in town today, I'd spoil you."

A sudden unexpected burning started behind Easton's eyes. He really loved Trace. "I know you would, baby. Don't worry about me. I have a full day planned."

"Doing what? Working? That's not a birthday."

Easton rubbed his chest, ignoring the pain while trying not to look too hard at things. "I like working. Speaking of which, I have to run. I plan to make a quick delivery before I go in today. You have no idea how much I miss your face. Please say you'll see me soon, even if it's a lie."

"I promise you'll see me soon." Trace sounded so serious that a lump formed in Easton's throat.

"I love you, nephew."

"I love you too, sweetie."

Easton slipped his phone into his pocket and gathered the boxes again. He ignored the wave of sadness that came from nowhere. Nico had to go to work super early and hadn't stayed the night as Easton had become accustomed to him doing. That was fine. Easton hated that Nico also hadn't asked Easton to stay with him. Judging by the heated kisses he'd left Easton with, Easton hadn't started worrying Nico was getting tired of him until this morning. After a rough night of bad dreams and even worse sleep, Easton had ended up staring at the ceiling and questioning every word Nico said before he left. He had seemed...secretive. Fuck. Now Easton worried that he had someone else, on top of being tired of Easton.

While scowling at nothing, Easton turned the knob with the tips of his fingers while fighting the boxes and hip-checking the door hard enough to leave bruises. He spilled out the front door, nearly tossing muffins through the air in his aggravation.

A sexy chuckle caressed Easton's ears, tightening the muscles in his stomach. "Damn. My sexy birthday boy looks fierce today. Tell Nico how to fix it."

Easton had to take a breath. Happiness made him winded. "Hey." Even to Easton's ears, he sounded breathless. "I didn't expect to see you this morning. I thought you had to work."

Nico easily took the boxes from Easton with one hand while using his free arm to pull Easton against him. "I had to go in super early, so I'd be free to do this," he said, dipping his head and claiming Easton's lips.

Easton melted in Nico's hold. The way Nico kissed him deep made Easton's heart skip a beat. He fought the urge to squeal and cheer. Nico turned him into a high school girl.

Nico pulled away and kissed Easton's forehead. "You should know I would find a way to spend as many seconds as I can with you on your birthday. I brought your favorite car so I can drive you to your regular visit with the nurses and then to work. No way will I let you slip by me today."

Easton pinched his butt for the insinuation. "As if I ever try to slip by you."

Instead of jumping away from Easton's abuse, Nico moved closer. "*Mmmm.* Hurt me, baby."

The luminous smile pulling at Easton's lips was out of his control. "Later."

Nico's eyebrows rose in a way that made Easton laugh. "I can't wait." On that note, Nico linked fingers with Easton and headed for the car.

Easton fought the urge to skip like a child. He'd never been this happy in his life. All the way to the hospital, Nico swapped between toying with Easton's fingers and bringing Easton's hand to his mouth to nibble on. Easton's cheeks hurt from smiling.

"Damn. They're busy," Nico muttered as he pulled into the hospital's parking lot.

"Yeah. This place is always packed. They have valet parking available. That's the only way I can ever get a spot."

"Nobody drives my baby." Easton bit his bottom lip at Nico's growled words, fighting a smile. Nico had let him drive after only their second meeting. He loved all the ways Nico made him feel special. "How about this," Nico said, pulling Easton from his happy daydreaming. "I'll drop you at the door and then park at that medical center across the street. Is that okay?"

"Sounds good," Easton said, gathering his boxes so he could exit quickly.

Nico pulled up to the door. He leaned over and gave Easton a quick kiss. "I'll be fast."

"I'll wait here," Easton promised as he slid from the car. He moved to the sidewalk and out of the way of anyone coming or going while he waited for Nico. It was a hell of a trek from the medical center to the hospital. Easton mentally prepared himself for a long wait.

"Easton?"

At the sound of his name, Easton turned his head and swallowed a groan. In the past year, he'd somehow managed to avoid running into his ex, Marcus, when he visited the nurses who'd cared for him. Marcus was a surgeon and at the hospital on a regular basis. Easton had known it would only be a matter of time before they saw each other again. "Marcus."

Marcus was blond and polished. Everything about him screamed money, from his fake tan to his unnaturally white teeth. He even smelled expensive. Marcus' smile kicked up a notch as Easton said his name. "What brings you here? Is someone sick?"

Easton shook his head. Even to Easton, his smile felt forced. "No. I'm bringing snacks to the nurses on the third floor who took care of me last year."

At Easton's claim, Marcus' gaze sharpened. He openly eyed Easton's scars, going as far as to sweep Easton's hair away from his temple to get a better look. Easton's heartbeat pulsed in his ears. He fought the urge to snarl and snap like a wild animal. The only thing stopping him was his hands were full, and he hated scenes. Before the attack, he'd kept his hair short. In the past year, he'd let it grow past his chin, and kept it shaped into a stylish mess. Not only had he come to like his hair, it also hid most of his scars from people like Marcus. "I could probably fix most of this. You wouldn't be able to tell anything happened once I finished." Marcus was a gifted plastic surgeon. People came all the way from the east coast and sometimes other countries just to have work done by him. Easton wasn't one of those people.

"Thanks, but I'm good the way I am."

Marcus' expression changed. His smile disappeared, replaced by open confusion. "That's an odd choice to make under the circumstances. I hope you're not choosing to cling to your scars just to avoid me." Like there weren't any other surgeons or men on the planet.

Easton fought the urge to snort at the guy's arrogance. "No. It's just not that important. I have a business that needs me, and surgery takes unnecessary time away from that. Not to mention, anyone who's bothered by a few scars doesn't need to be in my life anyway." Yes, it was a low blow. Marcus had dumped him a few short hours after the attack. Easton was no longer arm candy in Marcus's mind. Easton's feelings had never been part of the equation.

The way Marcus's face hardened let Easton know his shot hit its mark. "Maybe. Or perhaps you're punishing yourself for all the times you've used your looks to pay your way. So who's the dumb bastard that's funded a business for you? I know you didn't pull that off by yourself."

If Easton hadn't spent almost a solid year

working eighteen-hour days to make his bakery a success, he might've been insulted. The thing was, he had worked his ass off and knew it. While his brother-in-law had financially backed him, Easton had repaid Flynn with interest in no time. No one had handed him that. "I'm sure thinking that helps you sleep at night after the way you ended things, but you needn't bother creating scenarios for me in your head. The truth is, I've never needed anyone to take care of me. I've always just preferred the company of older men." Men like Marcus, but that went without saying. "It's too bad you couldn't see that while you had a chance." Easton hoped Marcus spent the rest of his life wondering if Easton had really cared about him. He hadn't, but neither had Easton been using him. Marcus was simply someone Easton had known his parents would approve of him dating and he hadn't liked being alone. Now, he gave no fucks what anyone thought about anything at all. Nor did he mind keeping his own company. This was the one life he'd been given, and Easton intended to spend it doing whoever and whatever he wanted. No one else's opinion need apply.

"Are you ready, *Knuddelbärchen*?"

Easton's real smile reappeared as Nico's hand slid across the small of his back. His life was different now. He wouldn't waste another second on people like Marcus. His gaze slid Nico's way. "Yes. That didn't take anywhere near as long as I expected." He headed for the door with his gaze locked on Nico and without bothering with goodbyes.

"Here let me carry these," Nico said, taking the boxes from Easton. "A spot opened before I made it to the other lot. Who was that guy?"

Easton shrugged. "Just a guy who goes to my parents' country club." Easton knew Marcus was still within earshot and didn't care. Marcus wasn't important and the shitty way he'd dumped Easton hadn't broken him. He had Nico now. The past no longer mattered.

"I can't believe you're working on your birthday." Nico tried to sound stern rather than whiny. It was all for show anyhow.

Easton's sexy eyes flashed with humor. "Awww, sexy. It's just for a couple of hours." He scooted closer, leaning across the car and snagging Nico's shirt. He slowly towed him closer. "Then you'll come get me at lunch. We'll go eat and then back to your place." His smile grew naughtier by the second before he kissed Nico. Nico's heart turned over in his chest. Damn. He had it bad.

Nico sighed. "Very well." He opened his door.

Easton stared at him, looking more than a little surprised. "You're going in?"

"Of course, *Knuddelbärchen*. Your brother is back in town, ja? He's working today too, right? It's time we meet."

"Are you being serious?"

Easton's open disbelief gave Nico pause. "Is there a reason I shouldn't?"

A smile exploded across Easton's face. "No. It's just that nobody has ever made the effort to meet Jake before. Of course, he would've hated anyone I dated, but I think he'd like you."

"Good. I'll walk you in."

Easton scrambled from the car. Nico bit the inside of his cheek to keep from laughing. He loved making Easton happy. It was the highlight of his day. Nico linked fingers with Easton and tried to act casual. Easton turned to say something as Nico opened the door to the bakery for him.

"Surprise!"

The chorus of voices screaming at once made Easton jump. His gaze shot to the open doorway. A myriad of emotions crossed Easton's face. "Holy shit."

"Language," a woman with ash blonde hair fussed as she stepped forward and kissed Easton's cheek.

"Mom. What are you doing here?"

Easton's open disbelief still hadn't faded.

Jake took over, towing Easton all the way inside and hugging him. "Happy birthday."

"What the—" Easton muttered. His head turned side to side as he took in all the people and decorations. "How did you do all this?"

"I didn't."

At Jake's claim, Easton blinked. His grip never loosened on Nico's hand. "You didn't? Surely, Mom..."

Jake shook his head. "This is all Nico. He put everything together. I just made some calls."

Easton looked his way. He looked shell-shocked. Once again, he opened his mouth the speak, but was interrupted as a young guy tackle-hugged him. Easton squealed, finally releasing Nico so he could squeeze the guy back. A hint of jealousy slapped Nico. He didn't know who the boy was, but he was the definition of beauty. It wasn't just the way he looked. It was his smile and the way he carried himself. The boy knew his worth and carried himself with that confidence. His smile bled wicked intent. He looked like sex on two legs.

"Oh my gosh. Trace. I can't believe you're here. Did you really make the trip for me?"

"Of course I did. You're my favorite uncle."

"I'm your only uncle," Easton countered with a laugh.

Trace's unusual blue gaze slid Nico's way. "Nico. Right?"

Now that Nico realized he was family, his jealousy was replaced with appreciation. Easton obviously cared about this boy and he'd apparently made a trip to be here. That meant a lot to Nico because it meant something to Easton. "Right. I'm glad you were able to make it."

Trace flashed Easton a wicked smile. "Damn, Easton. He has an accent too. Look at you go."

Easton blushed. Nico swore his stomach growled as he watched the blood rise to Easton's cheeks. Hunger owned him every bit as much as Easton did.

"Whoa," Trace muttered, bringing Nico's gaze his way once more. He watched Nico closely, obviously taking in Nico's every reaction to Easton. "This one is a keeper," Trace said out of the corner of his mouth to Easton.

The move had Nico shaking his head and smiling. The boy was a mess.

Easton seemed immune. "I know." His chirped response had Nico's smile growing even wider. He didn't even complain when Trace dragged Easton away to talk to someone else.

Nico held his ground and watched. Keeping an eye on Easton from a distance was his specialty. He'd done this just to see the happiness he now witnessed. All Nico wanted was to enjoy the show.

"I'm Flynn."

Nico glanced over at the thick Scottish accent. A man with red hair so dark it looked like it was brown stood at his side with his hand extended. Nico accepted his handshake. "Nico."

"Jake told me. I'm his husband, Easton's brother-in-law."

"I've heard the name," Nico admitted.

Flynn motioned toward a pair who stood nearby. Nico already knew one was Easton's mom. "These are Easton's parents, Jim and Patricia."

Nico shook both their hands. "Nice to meet you."

They exchanged pleasantries openly eyeing one another. Money and high society bled from their pores. He recognized Patricia from her run for governor. Easton looked more like his father than his mother, but he had her eyes. Nico wanted to like them for that reason alone. The trouble was, Nico rarely liked anyone. He wasn't overly friendly. Nico had spent his life learning to fight. Confrontation lived in his blood. He had to work at being nice.

"You look familiar to me," Jim said, breaking the ice.

"He should," Flynn said with a laugh. He glanced Nico's way. "How many heavyweight boxing titles have you won?"

"Seven." Nico kept his voice even and free of pride. Even though he was proud of those titles, it wasn't for the reasons people would think. Winning meant freedom from a life he'd desperately wanted to escape. Those titles opened doors and gave him opportunities he wouldn't have otherwise.

"Wow," Patricia said, drawing his gaze. "I really don't know much about sports, but that sounds like it took a lot of work. That's something I appreciate."

Nico dipped his chin, acknowledging her praise. "Thank you. I started training very young."

"Where are you from originally, Mr..."

"Braun. Nicolaus Braun. You may call me Nico. Everyone does. I was born in Hesse, Germany."

"That's one of the most impoverished places in Germany, isn't it?"

The fact that she knew that was disturbing. "Ja. My family now lives in Wolfsburg." Thanks to his money and their agreement to stay as far away from him as possible.

Patricia face cleared. "Oh. You must take care of them. That's good."

Nico was fairly certain there were insults hidden in there somewhere, but he didn't care enough to go digging for them. It was also possible Patricia was just painfully straightforward, which was fine by him. He would be the same. "Taking care of people is what I do."

Jim and Patricia both smiled—like he'd said exactly what they wanted to hear. Flynn slapped him across the back and used the motion to rescue Nico by steering him toward where Easton stood. "I'm going to introduce Nico to my son." Nico didn't bother pointing out they'd met. He nodded and moved along, thankful for the reprieve. "They're trying," Flynn said as soon as they were out of earshot. Flynn stopped short of Nico's goal. Nico stopped too, since it was obvious Flynn had something on his mind, but Nico's gaze stayed with Easton. He looked so happy and animated today.

Trace stood leaned against another man's chest. He had a sucker in his mouth and still looked as wicked as before, but now Nico saw what the other half of his life looked like. His man looked lovesick and satiated—like he was well loved in return. Nico smiled at the sight.

"I know who you are." Nico's gaze snapped to Flynn's at the announcement. Flynn's expression was the same friendly one as before, but Nico was still certain he'd heard right. Flynn gave him a sharp nod. He made a sweeping motion toward the room in general. "But you did all this, and I haven't seen Easton this happy. Not ever. I think you care about him and your intentions are good. You just need to know that I know and I'm watching."

Nico dipped his chin. "Fair enough. Who is this man with your son?" Nico asked, moving to what he hoped was safer ground.

"His husband."

Nico blinked. "Trace doesn't look old enough to have a husband."

A smile exploded across Flynn's face. "He's grown. Don't tell him I said that, but he is. I also got married very young. We're a loyal bunch—like wolves. We find the one for us and mate for life. You've been good for Easton," Flynn tacked on to the end as if trying to sneak the return to their earlier subject past him. "The past year has been rough. Easton has stayed glued Jake's side for most of it. Then we went out of town and come back after a few weeks and you've completely turned him around. I'm impressed."

"You'll probably think this is crazy."

"Oh, I think all this is crazy," Flynn said, interrupting him. "But I'm the last person who should be throwing that word around."

"I love him."

Not an ounce of surprise marred Flynn's features. "Good. That makes more sense than anything I imagined this to be. You should come meet my son-in-law. He thinks I hate him. It's hilarious."

Recognizing the inquisition was over, Nico accepted the reprieve and headed Easton's way. His heart didn't beat correctly until he drew Easton back against his chest. Easton was mid-story about the carnival. He kept talking even as he stroked Nico's arms around his waist and Nico kissed the top of his head. As long as Easton was happy, Nico didn't give a damn about anything else.

"Hey, baby," Easton said, sounding breathless and making Nico realize he'd finished his story.

"*Knuddelbärchen.*"

"Oh. Wow. You're Nicolaus Braun." At Trace's husband's remark, Nico met the man's stare. He looked nice—like a man who would stay loyal. "I saw you fight a few years back in Vegas. It was amazing. A little aggravating because tickets were like a billion dollars, and you knocked Sammy Tracey out like five seconds in, but still. That was amazing. I'm Hunter, by the way."

Nico let go of Easton long enough to shake Hunter's hand. "Please call me Nico. Thank you for agreeing to make the trip for this. It means a lot to Easton, and since it means a lot to Easton, it means a lot to me."

Hunter nodded. "No worries. Trace loves his family and I live to make him happy. Good job, by the way, putting all this together."

Nico nodded. He liked Hunter. "Flynn doesn't hate you."

"Hey," Flynn said, laughing. "Be careful with the secrets, lad."

Easton shook with laughter. The sensation against his chest was the best feeling in the world. Nico needed a moment alone with him. Just one. Then he would share Easton again. "Is it okay if I steal Easton? I'd like to give him his gift."

Trace waved them away. "No. Go. Easton needs gifts. In fact, this will give us time to get everyone gathered around the gifts in here so he can open them when you get back."

Nico dipped his chin. "*Danke.*"

Of course, he should've known Easton would balk. "You gave me my gift yesterday."

"No," Nico said, leading Easton to the door. "That was a trinket because I felt like giving you something pretty. Today is your birthday. It's a big day. Let me make it special because it matters to me."

He felt Easton deflate. "Okay."

Nico smiled and shook his head at Easton's defeated tone. It was like he wasn't about to get a kickass gift or something. The moment they stepped outside, Easton faced him, waiting. Nico's smile grew. Easton might pretend he didn't want anything, but Nico knew better. He was curious and excited. Nico dug into his pocket and pulled out a key ring. He held it out to Easton. "The Mustang is yours. I signed the title over. It's in the glove box."

Easton's gaze moved between the keys and the car and back again. He didn't reach for the keys. "No, Nico. You said that car is your baby, and *it's a fucking car*. You can't give me a car."

"*You* are my baby. I can do as I please. There are twelve more cars in my garage. This one is yours."

"Nico." There was a hint of desperation in Easton's voice now.

Nico didn't back down. He took Easton's hand and put the key in his palm. "If you don't accept my gift, I'll be hurt. You do not wish to injure your grumbly bear."

Easton's shoulders fell. "Nico."

"Stop saying my name. My mind won't be changed. Now thank me and tell Nico he's amazing."

A snort of laughter escaped Easton. "You are amazing, but—"

"No. Tell me how much you love it."

"I do, but—"

"No," Nico said, ensuring Easton understood it would be the last *but* he heard. "You will kiss me now and say nice things."

Easton laughed and shuffled closer.

Nico tapped his lips.

With a shake of his head, Easton went up onto his toes. Nico bent so he could reach him. The moment their lips met, Nico swept him closer, crushing Easton to his chest. Easton buried his face in the crook of Nico's neck. "You're the greatest person I know. I'm not upset about the present. It hurts my heart that I can't do as much for you as you can for me, but I want to."

Easton was wrong. He did more for Nico than he ever imagined. Easton existed. He breathed the same air as Nico. Nico wasn't empty anymore—the way he'd been every day until the first time he'd set eyes on Easton. Some things were worth more than all the money in the world. Nico could buy all the materials things for himself. Easton was priceless. "Kiss me again," Nico begged. "Then I will be the most spoiled of men." It was the God's honest truth.

———

EASTON'S ENTIRE BODY HUMMED WITH happiness. Nico had thrown him a surprise party. Jesus. He couldn't get past it. No one, including his parents, had ever done something so amazing. Nico should've stopped there. Giving him the car was too much. Easton needed Nico to understand he didn't care about his money. Accepting a car made him look like a gold digger. He'd know. It wasn't his first time getting a car. It hadn't ended well last time. Easton didn't want things to end with Nico at all. Unfortunately, Nico seemed pretty dead set about Easton accepting his gift. He'd have to find a different way to stand his ground—like spend a fuck ton of money on Nico. The thing was, Easton didn't have a fuck ton of money. But his parents had given him a nice-sized check for his birthday. Easton could spend that on Nico. He didn't need anything else. Easton stared into space, making a list of ways to spoil Nico in his mind.

The door opened and Marcus sailed in, making Easton's mind go blank. Twice in one day was too much. "Marcus?"

The too-white smile flashed his way. "Hey, darling. The third-floor nurses were kind enough to share their muffins and tell me all about your bakery. I had to come see for myself."

"Oh. Well, now you've seen." Easton tried not to sound unwelcoming, since—technically—Marcus was currently a customer, but damn. This was too much.

"I also forgot until after you'd walked away that today is your birthday."

"Okay." His discomfort grew by the second.

He set a card in front of Easton and claimed a barstool opposite him. Easton didn't reach for the card. He couldn't stop staring at Marcus, waiting for the other shoe to drop.

"I've been thinking about our conversation

today." *Fuck.* "I think I owe you an apology." *Double fuck.*

"No. You don't owe me anything." Easton tried keeping his voice steady. This could not be happening.

"I do," Marcus argued. "When we were together, I assumed it was sort of a business arrangement. I took care of you financially, and you took care of me in a different way."

"Mhmm," Easton hummed noncommittally.

"Then you had your accident." Accident—like Easton had tripped and fell on some ice.

"Mhmm," Easton hummed again, trying to wrap his head around some bullshit. Nope. He wasn't going to make it. Sitting quietly and being pretty didn't quite fit him anymore. "I wouldn't quite call being kidnapped from a parking lot, tortured, raped, and then left for dead outside a club an accident, but okay. I'm still listening."

Marcus looked away as if he found Easton's words distasteful. Easton almost laughed. If Marcus couldn't hear it, he sure as hell wouldn't have survived it. Marcus squared his shoulders and met Easton's stare again. "See, that's exactly why I owe you an apology." As Easton had said, he was listening. "When your father called and said you'd been found in the back parking lot of Club Fusion, I thought maybe you'd been out partying, and someone had slipped something in your drink. It never occurred to me you'd been taken from somewhere else and dumped there."

"Mhmm." Easton really couldn't stop. He heard the condescending sound each and every time he made it, but he just couldn't stop.

"I mean, you used to hang out at that club all time. The news that things had been much worse didn't make its way to me until it was too late to take back what I'd done. I realized today that—late or not —you deserve an apology." Marcus kept talking about an apology without actually making one and Easton wasn't feeling it.

"Was that it?"

Marcus smiled at Easton's smartass tone. "I'm sorry."

Well, it was better than nothing. "Water under the bridge."

Marcus brightened even more. "I'm glad to hear you say that. May I ask, are you dating that guy I saw you with today?"

Easton bit back a laugh. "Yes."

"Seriously?" Marcus sounded every bit as disbelieving as Easton expected.

"Yep."

Marcus pulled a face. "I can't imagine your parents approving of such a match."

Easton's smile grew by the second, because he knew lots of things Marcus didn't. One thing in particular—Nico was standing behind him. "Actually, they love him."

"Really?" Marcus couldn't have sounded more skeptical if he tried. "You should really consider taking me back. I can't imagine why they'd want you with someone like that."

Nico trapped Marcus against the bar. His massive arms flexed on either side of Marcus. He looked deadly—like he was an inch away from murder. It was fucking hot. Nico spoke close to Marcus's ear. His deep voice sounded like the devil had come calling. "They love me because I'm a seven-time heavyweight champion, which means I'm swimming in money and can take care of their son, even though he doesn't need anyone to take care of him. You should hate that I'm a seven-time heavyweight champion, because I'm about to use my skills to snap your fucking neck."

Easton fanned his face. He was totally sucking Nico's dick the second they were alone. Hell, he might not make it that long. He bit his lip to stop a moan from escaping.

"I only came to wish Easton a happy birthday." Marcus sounded ridiculously calm for someone who was about to die.

"Then say it."

Marcus focused on Easton. "Happy birthday."

"Thank you," Easton said graciously.

"Now, choose to leave with both your legs still working all on your own with nothing else to say."

"Yep," Marcus said, slipping from the stool and disappearing.

Easton didn't watch him go. He couldn't stop staring at Nico. Nico's gaze never wavered from Marcus until he was out the door. He focused on Easton. His expression shifted from murderous to concerned in an instant.

"Are you okay?"

Easton nodded.

Nico didn't look convinced. "Are you sure? Your face is red."

"I'm turned on," Easton admitted without an ounce of shame. "You have no idea how sexy you are. This has been my best birthday ever. Thank you for being amazing. I can't wait to have you alone."

"We should go to the car."

Easton nodded. "We should." He glanced over his shoulder. Julie worked the opposite end of the counter, filling up the trays in the display. "I'm leaving, Julie."

"Okay. I hope the rest of your birthday is amazing."

He flashed her a smile. "Thank you." When his gaze swung back Nico's way, Easton was nearly blasted off his feet by the heat in Nico's stare. Even with all the barely contained fire inside Nico, he still waited patiently for Easton to gather his things. As Easton walked toward Nico and Nico reached for his hand, a calm knowledge settled over Easton. This was real. Easton wasn't dating Nico to be dating someone—like he'd always done in the past. He didn't need Nico, but Nico was completely necessary to him. As their palms met and their fingers linked, Easton accepted the truth. Nico was the one.

SEVEN

EASTON: *I'm off work.*

Nico: *Good. You need more down time. I'm finishing up a job.*

Easton: *Can I come to you?*

Nico: *I'd love that.*

NICO SWIPED AWAY A SPECK OF DUST ON THE pristine sixty-six Shelby he'd just finished restoring. Its owner would be proud. Of course, with the guy's eighty-thousand-dollar budget, Nico had been able to go wild on making her perfect. He loved how she'd turned out.

"Nicolaus Braun." At the sound of his name in

such a condescending tone, Nico's head shot up. The tall, dark-haired figure trailing through his shop was an unwelcome sight, as always. Detective Whiskey Harris loved these unexpected visits as much as Nico loathed them. Still, he'd be damned if he let it show.

"Whiskey." Nico didn't give the man the courtesy of using anything other than his first name. Respect went two ways.

Light brown eyes focused on Nico. With his ridiculously long lashes and full lips, Whiskey might've been pretty if he wasn't such an asshole. "Have you seen any of your brother's friends around lately?"

"Have you heard from me?" Nico countered.

"Nope." Whiskey made the "p" pop. "That's why I stopped by. It's been a while."

"Has it?" Nico never gave Whiskey the satisfaction of getting under his skin.

"It has." Whiskey ran his finger along the lines of the car. "This is nice."

"It is. It's also worth more than you make in three years, so watch yourself."

Whiskey shoved his hands in the pockets of his khakis and focused on Nico. "It seems odd that you have so many customers with so much money to burn. It's almost like you're friends with the mob."

Nico's mouth lifted in one corner. Sometimes, Whiskey was funny. Everyone knew all fights, MMA and boxing, were mafia run. That was life. Everyone belonged to someone whether they saw their strings or not. "As hard as it is to believe, not everyone who has money is a criminal. But I don't ask questions either," Nico said with a laugh. "People bring the cars. I fix the cars. End of transaction."

Whiskey nodded as he circled the Shelby, eyeing the details while trying to scope the place on the sly. "So you say none of your brother's pals have come calling," Whiskey repeated.

Nico lost his humor. Easton would be along any minute and Whiskey needed to go. "You'd be the first to know, as you should know by now."

Brown eyes focused on him and didn't budge. They were hardened by—no doubt—seeing too much of the bad. "Maybe." Without another word, Whiskey headed for the door. Nico watched him go. He fucking hated this. Having Whiskey Harris in his life was the definition of no good deed going unpunished. Nico had unknowingly opened his home to evil once and now the taint followed him everywhere.

"Hey, sexy baby."

Nico blinked, wondering how long he'd been

staring at the spot where Whiskey disappeared. Easton stood in his place, looking happy and beautiful. Just as Nico always wanted. He shook off the darkness. "Sweet angel."

Easton's smile kicked up a notch as he crossed the garage. Even though Easton wore bright colors, Easton walked straight into Nico's arms, as if he wasn't covered in grease and dirt. His arms snaked around Nico's neck. He drew Nico down for a kiss. Their lips met and all thoughts of Whiskey and the devil disappeared. Easton wiped away all the ugliness, the way he always did. A hum vibrated around Nico's tongue as Easton shuffled even closer.

"Mmm, I've been waiting all day for that," Easton mumbled against his lips.

Nico deepened their kiss once more while kneading Easton's ass. Damn. He was enthralled with Easton. "Goddamn," Nico growled, hauling Easton flush against him. "I've been missing you."

The way Easton glowed made everything better. "Same. I have some news that should make you happy."

"Is the news that you thought about me kissing you all over all day?"

"I always think about that, but no," Easton said, laughing. "I hired another employee, and I gave Julie more hours so she can train the new girl. All this frees me to spend more time with you."

Nico fought the urge to crow. Instead, he put Easton first. "I'll cover her salary."

"Nope. I've got it. You're right. I work too much, and if I don't want to get burned out, I need to either cut the store's hours or hire help. So I hired help. Right now, things are going great and I can afford it. If things change, I'll cut store hours." He pulled an adorable face. "This is my first business. I'm still learning." He released Nico and glanced over at the car. "Look at this, though. Wow. You did so good, baby. I'm blown away by your talent."

Nico couldn't focus on a word Easton said. The way Easton glowed and sparkled was always a punch to Nico's chest. Sometimes, he thought there was no low he wouldn't stoop to keep Easton happy. Everything was gray when he wasn't around. Easton didn't realize what he gave Nico. Nico came from a dark place where no one smiled or said nice things. He'd been born into an angry family and then he'd fallen into a trap of fuckery and nightmares. Fame had meant nothing beyond the money. He'd never known real happiness. Then, light green eye had focused on him through a haze of blood and pain. Nico couldn't see anything else anymore. He'd kill anyone who came between them.

"You are beautiful. I see nothing else now that you're here."

Easton blushed, turning adorably shy. "I'm a mess after baking all morning."

Nico's gaze never wavered from Easton's face. If he had a speck of flour anywhere, Nico was blind to it. Nico couldn't even blink. Whiskey's visit had reminded him of all the bad and all he stood to lose. The pressure building in his chest was crushing his heart and lungs. Easton was the only good thing.

The way Easton shifted nervously had Nico trying to get his intensity under control. His emotions weren't listening. Easton tugged at the hem of his red shirt. His gaze bounced in every direction, trying to avoid Nico's burning stare. "Did I miss something?" Easton sounded so fucking nervous and Nico couldn't stop the growing desperation inside him.

It burst out in a way even Nico didn't expect. "I love you."

Easton's gaze jumped to his and didn't budge. All nervous motion stopped. Easton looked more serious than Nico had ever seen him. All bubbly charm slipped away. He was pure longing in human form, staring at Nico—like a sponge waiting to soak up everything Nico was willing to give. That was exactly why Nico loved him so fucking much, because—like Nico—Easton needed love. "Really?"

There was more hope in that one word than Nico had ever witnessed. "Yes. You are my *Knuddelbärchen*. I think I've loved you since the first time I saw you. It's too big for me to keep trying to hide it. I love you." Every time Nico said the words, the tightness eased in his chest.

Easton swallowed. "Will you believe me if I say I love you too? I think I have since the night we wished on the stars." He was too serious for Nico to think he was lying. Easton meant every word.

"I believe you." It wasn't a passionate moment. It was an honest one, which gave their words power they might've lacked otherwise. "You should stay with me tonight."

Easton nodded. Still, his gaze never wavered. "Whatever you want."

Whatever he wanted. Nico liked the sound of that. "I want you."

"I want you too."

Easton sounded calm. Steady. Still, Nico felt like he was pushing. "Do I ever scare you?" Nico knew he was too much. He never wanted Easton to be scared of him.

Easton shook his head. "I trust you."

He shouldn't. Nico was dangerous and a liar. In truth, he was a lot of horrible things, but not when it came to Easton. "We should go home."

"I'll drive." Easton headed for the door and Nico followed—like Easton had his heart on a leash. Nico wasn't ashamed to admit Easton completely owned him. There were worse things than being a lovesick fool. Nico would know. He'd already lived through damn near everything.

EASTON COULD FEEL NICO'S INTENSE STARE boring into his back. His heart raced for more reasons than one. Nico had said he loved him. Easton had said it back. He wanted to squeal like a little girl, but his body burned too hotly. Nico's body collided with Easton's back.

"Nico." Even Easton heard the pained desperation in his voice.

"I will fix you," Nico said, sweeping Easton off his feet. He veered to the left, heading toward his office.

Easton knew they weren't alone in the building. Nico had at least two workers there, but they didn't encounter anyone. It was as if they made themselves scarce. Once inside Nico's office, Nico kicked the door closed behind them. He set Easton on the desk. Easton couldn't look away from Nico's intensity. His jaw flexed. Easton stared at the blue eyes he loved so much while Nico focused on the task of unbuttoning and unzipping Easton's jeans. Easton lifted his hips as Nico tugged the lower half of his clothes down. With his bare ass perched on the edge of Nico's desk, Nico fisted Easton's cock. His expression nearly stole Easton's orgasm right then. Nico looked like he imagined the devil would when he received a new soul. Then, Nico stroked. Easton bit his lip to stop himself from crying out. He was already on the edge.

"I want to fuck you," Nico said, making Easton's vision blur at the edges.

Easton whimpered. He couldn't help it. "Please?"

"I don't have anything here. Nothing to ease things. I won't treat you like that. But you need release." Another whimper escaped Easton. Nico only toyed with the tip of Easton's cock. The teasing was merciless. Easton's hips kept leaving the desk, seeking more, but Nico wouldn't give it to him. Nico was mostly shaking the top two inches of Easton's cock rather than stroking—like he would while jacking off. It was just enough to make him half insane. Easton writhed. Nico watched. Easton's every breath was labored. He was dying. "You can do this." Fuck. Easton didn't even know what that meant. Then Nico stopped, and Easton thought about murder. Nico stripped away the bottom half of Easton's clothes. "Lean back, sexy. Spread those knees."

Easton leaned back on his elbows and spread his knees wide. Nico sucked two of fingers, wetting them before slipping them inside Easton's ass. He curled them and rubbed, massaging Easton's prostate as he went back to shaking only the tip of Easton's cock. Easton's mind was a mess. It didn't want to focus on any one thing. His body was on fire. He wanted to come.

"Nico. Jesus. Please?"

There was no mercy in Nico's eyes. "You're so sexy, Easton. You have no idea how you look to me right now. I'm ready to blow in my jeans from watching you."

Easton tried filling his lungs, but he couldn't. He was too fucking horny to breathe. "I can't." Even Easton didn't know what he couldn't do. Anything, he supposed. He wanted Nico's dick too much. "Please?" He couldn't stop begging. "I need you inside me."

"No. I won't hurt you. You can do this."

Fuck. Easton swallowed a growl. He didn't know what Nico thought he could do, but it wasn't happening. He was too fucking turned on to function. Pressure built. Easton tried fucking the tips of the fingers Nico barely stroked him with. His muscles tensed as he fought for the orgasm he couldn't reach. Frustration clawed at his skin and brain. He was almost there. It was just out of his reach. Then, Nico released him. A cry of denial reverberated from the walls. He thought he might physically fight Nico.

Nico pressed hard with his fingers—like punching a button inside him and stars popped behind his eyes. An orgasm slammed into Easton so hard, a silent scream ripped from his throat. He collapsed on the desk, twitching and incapable of stopping the involuntary spasms rocking his body. Nico kept punching that button over and over, taking Easton higher than he'd ever been. Words filled the air, coming from somewhere within his soul. Easton had no idea what he said, but it was all true.

When it was over, Easton's entire body shook

from the power of his orgasm. Even though he was a mess and his body was like gelatin, Nico gathered him into his arms and kissed him deeply. Easton's eyes filled with tears. He swore he could feel Nico's love like a physical touch caressing him.

Nico changed angles. "You're mine," he whispered before reclaiming Easton's lips. It was true. Easton couldn't deny it or care. Nico owned his soul and Easton was fine with it. After all, they'd made a fair trade. Nico was his.

EIGHT

CANDLELIGHT FLICKERED ACROSS THE MENU. Delicious scents filled the air. Pressure weighed heavy on Nico's brain, making his head pound. These moments hit without warning sometimes. Nico clenched his back teeth and fought against the oncoming panic attack. He'd been dating Easton for four months. Every day, at least four times a day, he'd look Easton's way and see the hands on the clock ticking. He couldn't lie forever. One day, Easton would learn the truth and he'd be gone. Nico couldn't take it.

"I love you."

Nico's gaze snapped to Easton's. His mind grasped the words but released them before Nico could retain them. He stared at Easton like an idiot, unsure of how to respond.

A huge smile stretched Easton's lips. Easton's knee bumped his beneath the table. "It's okay to admit you weren't listening," he said with a laugh.

Like that, the panic attack was gone. "I love you too." Nico smiled, feeling sheepish. "Sorry. I heard you. It was just one of those moments where my brain worked slower than I like."

With a chuckle, Easton glanced around the low-lit restaurant. "This place is nice. I thought it would be more crowded than this for its opening weekend."

Nico nodded. His gaze swept the room. Each table, covered in white tablecloths, had someone sitting at it. The place wasn't dead, but usually new restaurants had bigger crowds the first few months after opening. "Maybe it's the prices," Nico said, adding his two cents. The place was ridiculously overpriced for a selection of foods that didn't sound that great.

"Meh," Easton hummed, still looking at the menu. "The prices aren't as bad as the listings. Listen to this one: Linguine mixed with a combination of garlic shrimp, lemon, tuna eyeballs, and topped with red pepper flakes. What the actual fuck?"

"You might be able to ask for a version where it's

not staring back at you," Nico deadpanned, hoping to make him laugh.

Easton's eyes danced with laughter, warming Nico's heart. He glanced around again, wondering if they could make a break for it, or if someone would stop them at the door.

A familiar figure cut his way through the room, catching Nico's attention. He dropped his gaze to the table, hoping against hope he wasn't spotted. A shadow fell over them, killing Nico's chances of reprieve.

"Detective Harris. Wow. This is a surprise. I haven't seen you in forever," Easton said, coming to his feet and hugging the young detective.

"You look great."

Nico's chin shot up at the open interest in the guy's voice. Fear of the guy ruining his life aside, Easton belonged to Nico. The cop would never be seen again if he thought to flirt with Nico's man.

"Thanks. I'm feeling great." Easton reclaimed his seat at Nico's side. His hand slid across Nico's knee, as if reassuring him after the dude's flirting. Nico was only slightly mollified, especially since the young detective could ruin Nico's life with one well-placed word.

Then Whiskey opened his mouth and did

exactly what Nico feared. "I have to say, this is a surprise, seeing the two of you together. I guess tragedy makes for strange bedfellows." Nico stared hard at Whiskey, daring him to continue. The guy's light brown eyes didn't show a single hint of fear. Either he didn't care Nico could make him disappear, or he wasn't that smart. "In my job, I see all sorts of things, so I guess I shouldn't be so shocked."

"I don't know what you mean." The nervous laughter in Easton's voice didn't hide his obvious confusion.

Nico felt the hammer fall before Whiskey even opened his mouth. "I just meant with Nicolaus being Jörg's brother and all, I wouldn't expect the two of you to be... together," he finished lamely, as if he didn't know how to define what he saw.

A moment of silence fell. The entire restaurant seemed to decide in unison to stop talking. A heartbeat passed. Nico had a million thoughts in the span of a second. There was one that rang out louder than the rest. He wasn't ready for Easton to look at him with disgust and hatred.

When Easton responded, his voice turned cool, but it was directed at Whiskey not Nico. "I'm a surprising guy, I guess."

Nico's gaze moved between Easton and Whiskey and back again. Whiskey shifted from foot to foot, looking uncomfortable and like he'd been silently chastised. Nico was... confused. Easton had just been told he was sitting next to his attacker's brother. Yet he hadn't pulled away or flown into a rage. Nico sat in silence and waited for the other shoe to drop.

Whiskey rapped his knuckles on the table in a show of nerves. "Well, I just wanted to say hi. I didn't want to walk past like we're strangers."

Easton's tone brightened. "It's a good thing you didn't try. I would've tripped you."

At Easton's playful tone, Whiskey brightened again, obviously relieved to be out of the dog house. "Stop by the precinct sometime. I'm sure some of the other guys would love to see you doing so well."

"I'll do that," Easton said, still smiling. "Maybe I'll even bring the guys some of my cupcakes for their hard work."

"Your cupcakes?" Whiskey sounded genuinely interested and Nico thought he would scream. Easton fell into telling Whiskey about his bakery while Nico fought the urge to put his fist through the guy's face. He'd shattered Nico's life and now he wouldn't go away so Nico could explain. Fuck. The rage was real. It was all Nico's fault, of course. He'd been the one who'd lied by omission. At any time, he could've admitted Jörg was his brother. He could've explained he'd been the one to find Easton half dead in that parking lot while looking for his brother. Nico should've told Easton all about driving Jörg to the police station, forcing him to turn himself in and face his punishment. He definitely wanted Easton to know how bringing Jörg to live with him was one of the biggest mistakes of his life. Easton needed to know Nico had been the one who'd checked on Easton nonstop, watching him from a distance. Nico had been the one who'd found himself drawn a little more to Easton's light and will to survive every day until he'd finally given in and walked through the door of Easton's Bakery. That was all on him. Silence was his sin. He should own it. Nico fell down such a deep well of self-loathing that he didn't realize Whiskey was gone and Easton was back to reading the menu like nothing happened until he felt Easton stroke his knee again. Nico stared hard at Easton until Easton turned his head.

A sexy smile stretched Easton's lips. His eyes shone bright with the same happiness they had since Nico admitted to loving him. "Do you think they'd tackle us if we tried to leave? I don't know if I can stomach anything on this menu."

Nico sucked in a breath. It felt ragged. "I love you."

Easton's smile faltered a bit. "I love you too. Are you okay?"

The truth slapped Nico. Easton knew everything. He probably always had. Yet he'd given Nico a chance anyhow. All the times he'd stayed silent had been for nothing. But he wasn't the only one who'd not said a word. "How long have you known?"

Easton didn't play coy. Nico realized now that wasn't him. Easton was always straight with people. He didn't play games. If he was scared, he said it. If he wanted anything at all, he let it be known. This was no different. "Since you let me drive the Mustang that first time. When you told me where you worked, I knew then. The police who came to the hospital to take my statement told me the owner of your shop had found me and called 911. After your brother turned himself in, Detective Harris kept me posted. He said you'd forced him to confess, but no matter how hard they'd pushed, Jörg wouldn't give up the names of the two friends who'd been with him that night. In truth, even though it leaves me knowing the other two are still out there, I was grateful he pled guilty and took the full sentence to avoid snitching on his friends. That decision kept me from having to testify or see his face again. Plus, your brother was the ringleader."

Nico's eyes fell closed. In his heart, he'd known that. When his mother had begged Nico to bring Jörg to the States to get him out of the wrong crowd and Jörg had immediately found the wrong crowd here, Nico had known. It wasn't a matter of hanging with the wrong people. Jörg was the wrong people. He'd probably refused to give up the other boys' names because they could tell even more on Jörg than he could on them. Jörg had been saving his ass.

Easton kissed him. It was the sweetest brushing of lips, and it was enough to open Nico's eyes in more than one way. In spite of his silence, his guilt, and his family, Easton loved him.

One corner of Easton's mouth lifted. "You never brought it up." He paused and shrugged. "So I didn't see a reason that I should. That has nothing to do with us."

"You're so beautiful." Nico couldn't stop. "And amazing and strong. I'm damn lucky to have found you. There's nothing I would not give if I could change what my brother did."

Easton set his chin on Nico's shoulder. "Everyone is responsible for themselves. I'm not my brother and he's not me. The same is true of you. Did I wonder about your intentions when you first came around? Yes. But you've been good to me from the first moment and I don't think about your relation to him at all." He pressed his lips to Nico's shoulder and inhaled.

Nico lifted his arm and made room for Easton to scoot closer. With Easton tucked against his side, they looked at the menu together. Nico tried focusing on the words. He kept catching himself turning his face Easton's way and kissing his ear. Nico couldn't help it. He'd spent so much time scared shitless he'd lose Easton any moment and it had been for nothing. Nico should've had more faith in Easton. In truth, it wasn't Easton he hadn't believed in. Nico couldn't trust himself. When it came to Easton, if Nico lost him, he might do anything. Now he was free.

A wave of nervousness overcame Nico. He didn't have to worry about Easton finding out about his brother anymore. There was nothing standing in the way of what Nico wanted most—a life with Easton. He kissed Easton's temple, drawing strength from his scent while he picked a place to start. "I know you feel safe with your brother, but—if I asked—would you consider moving in with me?" Nico held his breath.

Easton didn't answer right away. When he did, he picked through his words, dousing Nico's hopes. "In the past, I've always moved in right away with whoever I was dating at the time. I was always at their mercy. It never ended well for me. I don't want things to be that way for us, and I have to start somewhere, so—for now—no."

Nico dropped his gaze to the menu. "Oh. Okay." Even he heard the disappointment in his voice.

Easton went back to staring at the menu too. After a moment, Easton spoke up. He sounded hesitant again. "I have to say, I'm surprised you asked. Usually, you tell me what I'm going to do, and I go along because I love you."

Nico loved this man and all his quirks. A smile tugged at his lips. He fought the urge to laugh. Easton didn't know how to give himself permission to make a decision for fear of making the wrong one. It was adorable. "Easton."

Easton turned his head and met Nico's stare. "Yes?"

"I'm moving your stuff to my house this weekend. It's my job to take care of you and I can do that better at my place."

"Oh. Okay."

Happiness penetrated every dark corner of Nico. He came to his feet, tugging Easton to his along the way. "Let's go. Eyes in our food is too far. We should hit up all the food trucks by the carnival. We're less likely to die of some mysterious food-related ailment there."

Easton was practically bouncing in place. "Yay. Star gazing."

"Rollercoasters," Nico corrected. "Then star gazing," he added, because no way in hell would Nico miss a night of holding his baby. Even though he now knew there was nothing standing in the way of him holding Easton every night for the rest of his life, he still looked forward to each and every opportunity.

NINE

FOR THE HUNDREDTH TIME, Nico stroked Easton's ass. He couldn't help it. It felt good in his hands. He honestly would've thought the longer they were together, the less he'd touch Easton. The opposite was true. In the six months since Easton moved in, Nico found himself doing more to always be with Easton, touching him. Loving him. Today was the perfect example. Easton didn't have to work, so Nico had created a reason for Easton to be at the shop with him.

"I thought I had a bottle of water around here," Easton said, sounding absent as he circled the Mustang.

Nico cast a halfhearted glance around the bay. "Maybe you finished it." He snagged Easton around the waist and kissed him. "I could wet your whistle, if you're thirsty."

A loud bark of laughter escaped Easton. He covered his mouth with both hands, trying to smother the sound before he obviously realized what he'd done and dropped his hands.

"Good boy," Nico praised, walking Easton backward and trapping him against the car. "I love your happiness and your laugh." He kissed him. "And you."

Easton's arms snaked around Nico's neck. "I love you too. Do you want anything to drink? I'll grab you something."

Instead of answering, Nico toyed with the zipper of Easton's coveralls. They were huge on him and they'd had to roll up the pants legs several times to make them work. Yet, Easton was still the sexiest man alive, even if he did look like a kid wearing his dad's clothes. Nico swiped his hand down Easton's back and cupped his ass again. "Go. Get hydrated and then hurry back."

Easton stole another kiss before slipping away to the office. Nico watched him go. He was sickeningly in love with Easton. It always grew bigger.

"Nicolaus Braun."

A sigh rose in Nico's throat at the sound of

Whiskey's voice. His gaze slid toward the bay doors. He watched as Whiskey picked his way through the tools and machinery until he reached Nico's side. "Whiskey," Nico said, hearing his dry tone and unable to stop it.

Whiskey leaned against the beat-up body of the 1956 Dodge Power Wagon Nico had recently acquired to play with on the side. He looked ready to stay awhile. Nico's gaze moved toward the office. Easton would be back any time now. The quicker they got this monthly visit over with, the better.

"What brings you by?"

For a moment, Whiskey stared into space, saying nothing. Nico figured it was some interrogation technique, but Nico had nothing to say. Finally, Whiskey sighed. "Just tell me one thing. This is completely off the record. I'm not a cop right now. This conversation never took place. I swear I'm not setting you up. This isn't about that. I just need to know once and for all. Am I wasting my time coming here? I'm never going to find those two boys, am I? Not alive anyway."

Nico stared at Whiskey in silence. He held the man's gaze and willfully refused to answer. Whiskey could claim all day that this was off the books, but Nico wasn't stupid enough to say the words aloud. But he let his face do the talking. Whiskey was wasting his time coming here. He would never find those boys. Not alive and Nico had ensured not their bodies either. Jörg was his brother. That blood tie had spared him. He'd spend the next fifty years in prison and then be deported if he lived that long. Those other two, Nico hadn't owed them shit, and they'd gotten no mercy.

Whiskey sighed and straightened away from the truck. "Okay. I guess there's no reason for me to keep looking. This is one of those few times justice was served, I guess."

Nico couldn't let that comment pass. "Justice would've been someone stopping those three before their evil ever tainted Easton's life. Justice would've been a police presence in this community," Nico said, pointing at the floor. "keeping people safe. Keeping Easton safe while he'd been minding his business, delivering cakes. A lot of people failed Easton that night, especially people like you. Maybe I was too late to save him from a nightmare, but I didn't fail him in the end. Maybe all that dogged determination you have to corner me would be better spent fighting for better protection for your people, rather than searching for lowlifes no one misses."

"My people, huh?"

Nico dipped his chin. His gaze never wavered from Whiskey's. "Yeah. Your people. I don't think you work this neighborhood for no reason. Neither do I think you stayed after Easton's case for so long on a whim."

Whiskey straightened his sleeves. "Maybe."

Nico fought a snort. He let it go as Easton strolled from the office, catching his eye. His heart skipped a beat. The way it always did when he looked at Easton.

"Detective Harris. I didn't know you were here." He looked down at himself. "I'd give you a hug, but my coveralls are dirty."

Whiskey looked more interested than he should. Nico considered putting out the man's eyes. "Easton. I didn't know you were here either."

Easton moved to Nico's side. Nico lifted his arm so Easton could slip beneath it. He held on to Nico's waist. "Nico is showing me how to change my oil and everything so I can take care of my car."

Whiskey's gaze moved down the line of cars in the garage. "Which one is yours?"

"Soon to be all of them," Nico answered for Easton, hearing the pride in his voice.

The way Whiskey's expression snapped closed

said he understood Nico's insinuation before Easton bounced in place. "We're getting married."

"That's fantastic." Whiskey couldn't have sounded less thrilled if Easton announced the man had just won a free colonoscopy.

His tone obviously didn't register with Easton. "If I send you an invitation, would you come?"

Whiskey rubbed the back of his neck. "Um."

Suddenly, Nico was enjoying the fuck out of himself. "Yes, Whiskey. You will come. Easton will be sad if you say no. No one makes Easton sad."

Easton nodded. "It's just a small gathering. You don't even have to get dressed up if you don't want to."

"He will get dressed up," Nico assured Easton, because this was fucking gold.

"Please," Easton said sweetly. "Even Nico's family isn't coming. We need a few people in the seats."

Whiskey's chest expanded on a deep breath. "Sure. I'll be there."

"Yay," Easton said, sounding adorable.

Whiskey shoved his hands in his pockets, looking uncomfortable. He cleared his throat. "Well, I guess I'll leave you two to your work."

"You'll hear from us soon." Nico smiled as he

made the claim because he couldn't force himself not to enjoy the man's discomfort.

With a sharp nod, Whiskey headed for the door. Nico watched him go until the man disappeared from sight.

"Why was Detective Harris here?" Easton asked the second they were alone.

Nico tucked Easton's hair behind his ear. He was so beautiful. Nico had to be a little honest. "He shows up at least once a month, because he thinks I have ties to the local mafia."

Easton scrunched up his nose the way Nico loved. "That's weird." His face cleared. "Wait. Do you have ties to the local mafia?"

They would be married soon. Easton should know. "Yes."

Without a single missed beat, Easton shrugged. "Everyone is owned by someone, whether they see the strings or not."

A smile exploded across Nico's face. He loved this man. "I'm only owned by one person." He crowded Easton against the car. "And he'll soon have my last name."

"Easton Braun," Easton said, staring into space with an awed air. "It sounds amazing, doesn't it?"

"It does." Nico grabbed Easton's ass and lifted

him from the ground. "When was the last time you made love on the hood of a car?"

"Four days ago," Easton chirped. "I still have the bruises."

"Backseat?"

"Agreed," Easton said, wrapping his legs around Nico's waist.

As Nico circled the car with Easton hanging from his neck like a monkey, he thanked every god for the life he'd been given. It hadn't always been pretty. In fact, sometimes his life had been downright messy. But the parts he shared with Easton made everything worthwhile. For the rest of his life, he would be worthy, and Easton would be happy.

Keep an eye out for the next book in the Sugar Daddies series, *Sugar Enforcer*.

Please consider leaving a review at the retailer where this book was purchased. Reviews really help with a book's visibility, which ensures I can continue writing. Thank you, Charity.

ABOUT THE AUTHOR

Charity Parkerson is an award winning and multi-published author with several companies. Born with no filter from her brain to her mouth, she decided to take this odd quirk and insert it in her characters.

*Eight-time Readers' Favorite Award Winner
    *2015 Passionate Plume Award Finalist
    *2013 Reviewers' Choice Award Winner
    *2012 ARRA Finalist for Favorite Paranormal Romance
    *Five-time winner of The Mistress of the Darkpath

Connect with her online:

--Join my street team: facebook.com/TeamCharityParkerson
    --Sign up for my newsletter: http://bit.ly/CharityNews
    --Website: charityparkerson.com

--Facebook:
facebook.com/authorCharityParkerson
facebook.com/TheMenofSin
--Twitter: twitter.com/CharityParkerso

www.ingramcontent.com/pod-product-compliance
Lightning Source LLC
Chambersburg PA
CBHW061244170626
46809CB00007B/2827